Zoe had just kissed her boss—again!

She should have felt worse about it, but didn't. She had fantasized about that kiss. Her mind told her not to do it, but she couldn't resist.

Now she knew what it felt like and wanted more. Much more.

Longing blazed a hot trail from her center up to her chest. Ethan pulled back and stared into her eyes.

"You're so beautiful." His breathless voice came as a whisper. "Tell me to stop." He kissed her more. She moaned. "I will if you want me to." Kisses. Ethan moaned into her mouth. Zoe felt the rumble in her belly. She moaned. "Tell me what you want," he groaned.

"You. I want you, Ethan. If you'll have me."

* * *

Intimate Negotiations by Nicki Night is part of the Blackwells of New York series.

Dear Reader,

Hey there! I hope you enjoy getting to know Zoe Baldwin and Ethan Blackwell. Have fun seeing the Big Apple through Zoe's and Ethan's eyes as their forbidden affair unfolds.

Zoe wants to take her career to a new level. She didn't let her last boss stand in the way of her advancement and she surely isn't going to allow her gorgeous new boss, Ethan, to stop her. However, they didn't plan on falling for each other.

Ethan likes Zoe's strong work ethic and innovative ideas. Zoe is an asset to his company. She's also completely irresistible. Zoe is smitten by Ethan's savvy, charm and good looks, making their work stimulating in more ways than one. Their desire for one another becomes too intense to deny until Zoe finds herself in a precarious situation that could put their relationship, reputations and careers in jeopardy. Find out how Zoe and Ethan navigate these *Intimate Negotiation*s. Enjoy the journey!

Ciao,

Nicki Night

NICKI NIGHT

INTIMATE NEGOTIATIONS

This book is dedicated to my husband
and best friend, Les, for showing me
what love feels like every single day.

ISBN-13: 978-1-335-23269-4

Intimate Negotiations

Copyright © 2021 by Renee Daniel Flagler

Recycling programs
for this product may
not exist in your area.

This edition published by arrangement with Harlequin Books S.A.

For questions and comments about the quality of this book,
please contact us at CustomerService@Harlequin.com.

Harlequin Enterprises ULC
22 Adelaide St. West, 40th Floor
Toronto, Ontario M5H 4E3, Canada
www.Harlequin.com

Printed in U.S.A.

A born-and-bred New Yorker, **Nicki Night** delights in creating hometown heroes and heroines with an edge. As an avid reader and champion of love, Nicki chose to pen romance novels because she believes that love should be highlighted in this world, and she delights in writing contemporary romances with unforgettable characters and just enough drama to make readers clutch a pearl here and there. Nicki has a penchant for adventure and is currently working on penning her next romantic escapade.

Books by Nicki Night

Harlequin Desire

Blackwells of New York

Intimate Negotiations

Harlequin Kimani Romance

Her Chance at Love
His Love Lesson
Riding into Love

Visit her Author Profile page at Harlequin.com, or nickinight.com, for more titles.

You can also find Nicki Night on Facebook, along with other Harlequin Desire authors, at Facebook.com/harlequindesireauthors.

Lord! Thank You for bringing me through this one more time. Let the glory be all Yours! I love writing and I'm so blessed to be able to indulge this joy. I want to thank everyone who inspires me just for being who they are. Thank you to Glenda Howard, Stacy Boyd and the entire Harlequin Desire team. Thank you to my fellow writing cronies who keep me inspired, Zuri Day, Lutishia Lovely, Tiffany L. Warren, Victoria Christopher Murray, ReShonda Tate Billingsley, Leslie Elle Wright, Sheryl Lister, Brenda Jackson, Beverly Jenkins, Donna Hill and so many more. To my heartbeats, Big Les, Little Les, Milan and Laila, you are my life. To my siblings, cousins, besties, readers, maniacs and book club buddies nationwide, thank you for being on this journey with me! Where would I be without your support? Like I said before, I dunno! You all rock!

One

"Well…better luck next time." Seth Sanders's tone was cool, almost frigid, and devoid of any concern.

Zoe Baldwin saw Seth's lips form into a smirk. He was gloating. She held her expression, hoping her true feelings didn't best her and spread across her entire face. "Yep." She offered a tight smile. "Next time," she said and then turned her attention to her computer. Chest up, back erect and eyes straight forward, she dismissed him.

She was done talking, even though she really wanted to lash out with stronger words. But she didn't want to come across as the bitter employee who didn't get the promotion. Yet, she *was* bitter. This was the second time she'd been overlooked, the second time an employee she trained was now getting the title she deserved, and Seth was instrumental in both incidences. Zoe couldn't prove it, but deep inside, she knew it.

Seth lingered for a moment before walking away. At

his exit, Zoe felt the threat of tears sting her eyes. She grabbed her cell phone and headed to the ladies' room. Going into the farthest stall, she bowed her head and let the tears fall. She hated that anger caused her to cry. Crying made her feel weak.

Zoe took a few deep breaths and then stood straight. She swallowed hard, pushing down other rising emotions. She closed her eyes, inhaled slowly and exhaled as much frustration as she could.

Seth's actions were nothing short of retaliation. She'd been one of the few women at Bowman Advisors who'd rejected his advances. She didn't care if he was the son of a board member. Seth was slick. He never made another pass at her but tried every single day to be just annoying enough to make her miserable at work. Most times she successfully ignored his childish behavior. But now he was standing in the way of her moving up the ladder. She didn't have enough evidence to actually prove it—yet.

Zoe took another deep breath and released it with conviction. Either Seth had to go, or she would. Her mentor had once told her that sometimes bosses fired employees but other times, employees fired their bosses. It was time to fire Seth.

She exited the stall, tucked her cell phone under her arm and washed her hands. She grabbed tissues from the box on the sink and dabbed her eyes. Studying her image in the mirror, she stared directly into her own doe-like eyes that matched her mother's, drawing strength from inside.

Zoe put a smile on her face. If she could handle the challenges of the life she lived, she could certainly handle the Seths of the world. With new conviction, she left the bathroom and dialed Willena Williams. Tough, brilliant and well respected, Willena was an icon in the finance industry. She was also one of Zoe's professors from grad school and had become her most trusted mentor.

"Good morning, Zoe." Willena's singsong voice was full and strong. It was one quality that allowed her to move a room full of people to silence or action. Zoe pictured her at her desk, the large office, the wall of windows behind her. She could see Willena in one of her tailored suits and her salt-and-pepper tresses cut low in the back and swinging over her left eye in the front. "Have a good weekend, my dear?"

"I did, but today…not so good. Can you do lunch?"

"Oh…lunch won't work but I can meet you for dinner. I haven't been to Smith's in a while. I could use a good steak."

"That would be perfect, Willena. Six o'clock?"

"Let's do five thirty."

"Great. See you then."

"Ta-ta for now" was Willena's signature sign-off. She even closed text messages with it, using TTFN.

Zoe headed back into the office feeling a tad better. She watched Seth eyeing her in his normal squinted fashion as she made her way to her cubicle. Zoe hoped the day went by quickly so she could get to her dinner with Willena.

Despite Seth's nagging presence, it did. The second the clock on her computer struck five, she shut it down, grabbed her purse and headed out the door. Again, Seth eyed her entire departure.

Maneuvering through the throngs of New York City's after-work crowd, Zoe walked at a brisk pace, the pace and rhythm that matched the soul of the city. It came automatically when she hit those streets. After a quick subway ride, she reached the restaurant with minutes to spare. Willena walked up seconds after her and in no time, they were being seated.

"Blue. Neat please, my dear?" Willena said to the waiter, asking for her usual Johnnie Walker Blue straight with no ice even before the server had a chance to place the menus in front of them. "And she'll have…" She paused for Zoe.

"I'll have Riesling, please," Zoe added.

"Uh!" Willena held up a finger just as the waiter was about to turn away. "Your best Riesling, thank you."

One day, Zoe would drink scotch like Willena, no ice, no chaser. Willena's drink choice was an indicator of the type of woman she was: aged, refined, hard and smooth at the same time, and of course no-nonsense. For now, Zoe was a white wine kind of woman.

"How's it all going, my dear?" Willena buttered a warm piece of bread from the basket on the table and took a bite.

"Okay." Zoe toyed with her bread, turning it over in her hand.

"Just okay? How's the family?"

"All are well. Stable. And yours?"

Willena had no husband or children to speak of. She'd been married to her work for more than twenty-five years, managing to maintain a few boyfriends along the way. She'd turned down her share of proposals. Instead, she was the proud, wealthy aunt who spoiled her tribe of nieces and nephews. "My nephew chose Harvard. Following in his auntie's footsteps. I'm so proud."

"That's great news! I know that makes you super happy."

"It certainly does."

Willena leaned aside for the waiter to place their beverages on the table. They took a moment to order appetizers and entrées.

"Now," Willena said, bringing the focus back to their reason for meeting once the waiter left with their selections. "What's going on at work?"

"I was passed over for a promotion—again."

"Hmm."

"This time stung worse than the last. I mean, at least the last time, I chucked it up to fair game. But this time, it feels…personal. Like sabotage. It's like they don't want me to move up in this company."

"Mmm-hmm." Willena nodded. Her lack of dialogue always propelled Zoe to talk more.

"Seth seemed happy that I didn't get the promotion." Zoe told her about their exchange this morning. "He's so inappropriate at times. I'm going to file a complaint, but I want to make sure the timing is right. I don't want to look like a sore loser." She took a deep breath, feeling the need to calm herself. "He takes joy in bugging me. I'm qualified. I deserve this."

Willena chimed in with a hummed response here and a nod there as Zoe continued to vent until their food arrived.

"You know that company is home base for the 'old boys' club,'" Willena said at last. "I think it's noble that you figured all you had to do was work hard and then you'd be rewarded." She shook her head. "Not there. If you don't have an in with the right executive or you're not family to one of the board, your chances of making it up the ladder are slim. But you knew that." She huffed. "You got what you needed from them. When other companies see them on your résumé, they'll take notice. It's time."

Willena bowed her head silently over her meal for a

quick grace. Her gesture reminded Zoe that she should do the same. Her mother would have reprimanded her had she picked up a fork without giving thanks first.

"You need to move on," Willena said when she looked up. "What's your plan?"

A plan. Good question. Zoe hadn't quite thought of one. She just knew it was time to move on. Hopefully she'd get a better salary. "I need a plan," she admitted.

"Yes. Spontaneity is best preserved for romance. Planning is imperative in business. We don't want to make rash or careless decisions about our career choices. Think about where you see your self in the next few years and make sure your next steps are ones that get you closer to that goal."

Zoe was glad she'd called Willena. She rarely volunteered her wisdom, but since Zoe had shared her situation, Willena had managed to give her the most thought-provoking advice in just a few words.

"In the meantime, I have a few friends in a few places." Willena always referred to her vast network of professionals with nonchalance. "You know Blackwell Wealth Management, right?"

"Of course."

"They're expanding. I'll ask Bill what the deal is over there. There may be an opportunity coming up with them. I'll keep you posted."

"I'd really appreciate that."

"In the meantime, work on your plan and send it to me. We'll see what the possibilities are for you."

Zoe nodded. Suddenly she felt lighter. Seth wasn't going to stand in her way of becoming all she was destined to be. Just because he didn't want to promote her didn't mean she wouldn't achieve her own career advancement.

"Now, about that love life!" Willena watched Zoe curiously with a raised brow.

Zoe threw her head back and laughed. "Willena! I'm fine."

"You have to have a *little* fun, honey."

"Mmm, this salmon is delicious!" Zoe tried to hold her smile back as she wrapped her mouth around a forkful and closed her eyes. When she opened her eyes again, Willena was still giving her the same raised-brow expression.

Zoe laughed again. She had no answer for Willena. She wasn't sure when she would ever be able to answer *that* question.

Two

"I just had the worst interview ever." Ethan palmed his forehead and sighed. "This guy was so arrogant you would have thought he was interviewing me to be his boss."

"Wow. Sounds like you've had some crappy candidates lately. I guess that vice president position is going to be mine after all?" his brother Carter teased him over the phone.

"I didn't say that. Don't go printing new business cards yet, bro. I've got three more interviews lined up for today alone! That VP job is mine."

"Wanna put a wager on it?"

"Nothing like a little friendly competition. What would you like to bet?"

Carter hummed. "Let's see. How about something really humiliating?"

"Ha! Don't do that to yourself. I'd hate to laugh at your pain when I win, but I will."

Carter laughed. "You mean when I win. Let me think…"

Ethan pictured Carter tapping his fingers on his desk while he thought.

"I got it!" Carter spit his words out so fast they startled Ethan.

"Okay. Whatcha got?"

"The loser buys the winner a brand-new set of Callaway irons."

"Ooo-wee!" Ethan sang. "That's a nice set of clubs. I could use those to beat you on the green again. Let's throw in a new golf cart, too."

"Aww. You want to buy me a cart, too?"

"Nope, it'll be you dipping into your savings for me. And I want my cart customized with some torque. Then I can ride over to your house with my irons just to hand you my business card with my new title."

"Um…excuse me… Mr. Blackwell."

Ethan's head snapped up. He noticed his assistant standing in the entrance to his office. "Yes, Bella?" Once the branch manager was hired, Bella would become the new office manager at that location.

"Your next candidate has arrived. A Ms.—" Bella looked down at the papers in her hand "—Baldwin. Zoe Baldwin."

"Okay. Give me two minutes and send her in."

"Will do, sir."

Bella left and Ethan returned to his call. "My next interviewee is here. Let's hope this one is better than the last one. I'll catch up with you later."

"Cool! And good luck. I'll send you some pictures of the clubs I want when you lose this bet."

"Ha! Later, big brother." Ethan ended the call and popped a mint in his mouth.

He wasn't exactly looking forward to the string of interviews ahead of him. The past few days of meeting with potential candidates to run the new branches of Blackwell Wealth Management in his territory had proven to be a bit exhausting. He and Carter had already swapped some interesting interview stories since their father put them to the task of expanding the company.

They were charged with opening several branches in each of their territories. Ethan was responsible for all of Long Island from the Cross Island Parkway to Montauk. Carter's territory included the five boroughs of New York City, and their colleague Dillon Chambers was responsible for expansion in Westchester County. Each held the position of regional director, and depending on how well they fared in the first six months, one of them would be selected to become the new vice president for the combined territories.

The position came with an impressive salary, new bonus structure and a corner office with a spectacular view of Lower Manhattan. And now that they had a bet going, Ethan or Carter would also end up with a whole new set of high-end golf clubs and a brand-new golf cart to go along with their bragging rights.

"Ready, sir?" Bella was at his door again.

"Yes, thank you. Send her in." Ethan closed his eyes for a quick moment and took a deep breath. *Please let her be normal.*

"Good morning, Mr. Blackwell."

The woman's voice went right through him. Ethan looked up. He stood slowly. Instinctively, he extended his hand at the vision approaching him. She was gorgeous. Gorgeous enough for him to have to actually think of the appropriate response to her *good morning*.

"Um. Yes. Good morning, Ms…"

"Baldwin. Zoe Baldwin."

"Yes." Ethan shook her hand and then put his hands in his trouser pockets.

Ms. Baldwin stood awkwardly for a moment. The silence between them suddenly rang in Ethan's ears like an alarm.

"Please. Sit." He gathered himself. "Do you have a copy of your résumé with you?"

"Yes, I do." She handed it to him. Ethan looked to see if she had a ring on her finger. She didn't.

"Great." He took the résumé from her and began looking it over, scanning the words but not reading a thing.

He had already decided he couldn't possibly hire this woman as his branch manager. One look at her and he barely remembered his name. Protocol and decorum abandoned him. This wasn't good. He was a professional. A professional that was accustomed to beautiful women, at that.

"Mmm-hmm." He pretended to take in the skills and credentials listed in the document. It could have been written in Greek for all he knew. He cleared his throat and focused harder, finally taking in her qualifications. Impressive. A few more moments passed.

Ethan placed the résumé down in front of him and sat back. "Why Blackwell Wealth Management?"

"Your history over the past decade has been quite impressive, despite a few hiccups here and there," she began. "You seemed to have responded quite well to the challenges you've faced and instead of just surviving, you thrive as a company. You have a record of unprecedented growth, yet you've managed sustainability extremely well, as well as double-digit growth."

Zoe seemed to warm to her topic, exuding calm and ease as she spoke. "Financial media used to have you on the one-to-watch but now list you as one of the best companies to trust your assets with and work for. Your employees and your clients rate you well. That reputation doesn't come by chance or good luck, but by great people leading great teams and lots of hard work."

She lifted her chin. "I'm a hardworking team player and a good learner with proficiency in the areas you're seeking. I'm also well-educated and smart enough to interact with amazing mentors who are extremely knowledgeable, well connected and instrumental in helping me navigate my career. I'm also very ambitious and believe I can truly be an asset to the company by helping you reach your goals. I'm looking forward to joining a solid team and continuing to develop and grow in this field, and I believe Blackwell is a great place to make that happen."

Zoe ended her response with a confident smile. Confidence. Not smugness.

Ethan almost didn't know what else to ask. She'd said all the right things. He wanted to shout, *You're hired.* Instead, he nodded, reviewed her résumé further and asked a few pointed questions about the different positions she'd held.

Each response was better than the last. Ethan was truly impressed. He could already see her leading a branch and possibly even taking on his role once he was promoted to vice president. Smart *and* beautiful. So what *was* wrong with her?

"Do you have any questions for me, Ms. Baldwin?"

"Yes. I have a few. With rumors stirring about a po-

tential recession, what is Blackwell's strategy for pro-
tecting the interests of the company, your employees
and clients, as well as their assets?"

Whoa! She's good. "That's a great question."

Ethan went on to speak to the organization's strategic
goals and explain why despite the rumors of a recession,
this was also the right time for the company to expand.

Zoe took notes as he spoke and asked a few more
poignant and thought-provoking questions. As her lips
moved, Ethan found that he needed to concentrate to
focus on her words. He shifted in his seat several times
to keep from staring. The last thing he wanted to do
was come across as inappropriate or make Zoe feel uncomfortable.

Ethan was sure one of the challenges she had refer-
enced was the sexual harassment issue they had dealt
with a few years back. Blackwell had addressed the report immediately, taken a strong stance against harassment and implemented changes to avoid future cases,
but not before the media had gotten a hold of the news
and published several scathing headlines. It took some
time for the company to recover from that stain. They'd
put in the necessary work to ensure their employees'
safety and rebuild their brand.

Ethan answered her last question about the next steps
in the hiring process. When she confirmed that she had
no more questions, he stood. "Impressive. If you're selected to advance to the next round of interviews, we'll
be in touch."

"Thank you, Mr. Blackwell. I hope to hear from you
soon. I'm excited about the opportunity to work for
Blackwell Wealth Management and truly believe this
would be a mutually beneficial fit."

Ethan smiled. Again, she'd said the right thing.

"Thank you, Ms. Baldwin." He held out his hand. When he touched her, her palm felt as soft as he remembered from the top of the interview. He let go quickly and nodded. She turned to leave, and Ethan tried his best not to watch her walk out. Setting his focus on his desk, he shuffled papers aimlessly. When she exited, he plopped back into his chair.

Ethan sighed. She was the best candidate by far. But how could he hire a woman he could barely take his eyes off of? She was bound to be some kind of trouble.

He looked at his clock. He had fifteen minutes before his next interview. He made a few notes on her résumé and put it aside before checking to see who was scheduled to come next. Ethan went to the LinkedIn profile of the next candidate to look at their picture. He couldn't be thrown off by another stunning beauty.

Suddenly he laughed. It started as a chuckle. He laughed harder. He chided himself for his ridiculous behavior and chuckled more at how Carter would joke when he shared this with him.

With several more minutes to spare, he decided to check messages. He still needed a distraction. Zoe Baldwin dominated his thoughts. When he opened his email, her name was already at the top of his inbox. He clicked and read her email, thanking him for taking the time to meet with her and consider her for the position. She reiterated a few key points from the interview and wrote that she hoped to hear from him soon. She closed with a line about being grateful to her mentor, Ms. Willena Williams, for making her aware of the opportunity.

Smart woman. Mentioning that a respected professional like Willena Williams was your mentor could never hurt. Between that and the quick follow-up thank-you note, Zoe Baldwin was racking up points.

Perhaps, Ethan would have to figure out how to work alongside a beautiful woman that made him struggle to keep focus. He was an experienced man. Most of all, he was a professional. But there was something about Zoe Baldwin that would test him. He could feel it.

He thought a moment longer. He needed the right team in place to guarantee a win. Zoe could definitely be an asset.

This was his chance. He had to impress his father and get that promotion. Carter had an advantage that Ethan didn't have. Ethan had much more to prove to their *father* than Carter ever did.

Three

Zoe was on her fifth outfit. The four others she'd tried on were strewn across her bed. Twisting side to side in the mirror, she shook her head before removing her suit jacket yet again. She tossed that one across the bed, too, removed her pants and threw those on top of the pile.

She chuckled and told herself that her outfit mattered because it was her first day, that she needed to make a great impression and she wanted to look very professional. Some of it was true but the real reason she wanted to look her best was because of her new boss.

Zoe had to admit, Ethan Blackwell was one of the most handsome men she'd ever laid her eyes on. She wasn't trying to entice, but she wanted to look great.

There was something about Ethan. He was smart, confident, and sex appeal oozed from him. Her second interview with him had gone smoother than the first. She'd been determined to land the job, but she'd still felt like she had been crushing on him after she left his office the second time. For the next few days, he'd randomly shown up in her thoughts. When he'd called to offer her the job, the thought of being around him on a daily basis had almost made her weak in her knees.

Having never been boy crazy, she laughed at herself now. Why in the world did she feel like she was in high school, crushing on the cute popular boy? The truth was, while she had done her homework on the company, she had also done some research about her new boss. He was well respected and gave back to the community. He and his brother Carter were bachelors. They were also Blackwells, which meant that they were from a different world. Theirs was filled with privilege and pedigree. The only window she had into that exclusive world was her clients in financial management. And Zoe made sure they knew few details of her modest background.

She grabbed the navy blue pantsuit from the pile on her bed and put it back on with a soft pink blouse and matching belt. She slipped her stockinged feet into a pair of smart-looking navy pumps. With gold stud earrings and a link necklace to complete her look, she was ready for her first day of work at Blackwell Wealth Management. Assessing her choice in the mirror one last time, Zoe sighed.

"Let's do this, girl," she said to her reflection.

She pulled her designer tote over one shoulder and picked up her car keys. Unlike her last job, her new commute would require no more than a fifteen-minute car ride. Parking in the lot near her office was plentiful. No longer would she have to fight the rush-hour crowds on the commuter railroad and subway for an hour and a half to get to downtown Manhattan. Besides her impressive new salary, this was one of the best benefits of her new job. Well, that and having a ridiculously handsome boss to look at every day.

That was all Ethan was going to be for her: something nice to look at. Dating her boss was out of the question. She'd seen too many people's careers fumble for dating on the job—especially due to dating bosses. Zoe also knew that after a few weeks of working alongside Ethan, she'd get used to him and his good looks would no longer matter.

For now, looking forward to seeing him every day was sure to make work interesting. Besides, a man like Ethan had to have his pick of beautiful women on a daily basis. Zoe could imagine he probably had several that he was probably seeing all at once—perhaps enough ladies vying for his attention that he could pick one for every night of the month without repeating. She was also certain that those women probably came from similar backgrounds—a perfect one filled with enormous wealth and privilege. Zoe had neither and she was fine with that.

Before walking out the door, she popped a pod in her coffee maker and filled one of her spillproof travel mugs with her favorite dark roast and added a touch of French vanilla creamer. Instead of wearing a light jacket, she wrapped a pashmina around her neck to protect herself against the cool autumn air. Her blazer was enough to guard her from the slight chill.

"He's probably arrogant," she said to her reflection in her rearview mirror as she put her car in Reverse and pulled out of her designated parking spot at her town house complex.

"Arrogant and entitled," she continued assessing him, "from a model, privileged two-parent household."

The women at the job would probably make her sick

from their pining after him. That alone would make her want to steer clear of any man. She could already imagine the hushed talk of him throughout the office. She would never be party to that. Taking in discreet glances of him would be enough for her. She appreciated good-looking men but was never one to *need* a man.

Zoe's favorite playlist blasted through the car's Bluetooth system. She nodded to the rhythm as she navigated traffic along some of Nassau County's busiest streets. The commute took longer than the fifteen minutes she'd estimated and she was glad she'd decided to give herself just over a half hour to get to work. It was all the time she needed to get her mind ready for her first day.

This branch manager position had everything she wanted and needed. The compensation package was the best she'd ever received. She would soon have a fairly large team to manage and was ready for the challenge. She'd gleaned her management style from what she believed were the best characteristics of the bosses she'd worked under. She looked forward to being a fair, firm and motivating leader.

Her thoughts carried her all the way to the office. She maneuvered her car into one of the spots designated for Blackwell Wealth Management and headed inside.

Bella, the new office manager, guided Zoe to the office she would occupy. It was slightly smaller than Ethan's oversize corner office and situated right next to his.

Outside of her office, Zoe took in the modern company space with its open floor plan, crisp white workspaces and a common area that also served as a kitchen. Any wall that wasn't full of windows held abstract artwork with bright pops of color. Her eyes scanned the rows of empty cubicles that she would help fill over the next couple of weeks. She was excited about the task of having a hand in building the team.

Just as Bella finished helping her set up her laptop, they heard footsteps. Butterflies fluttered in Zoe's belly. Before she saw his face, before she heard his voice, she felt him. Ethan had arrived and set off the butterflies.

Moments later, he appeared in the frame of her office door, looking like a work of art himself. She tried not to but couldn't help taking him in slowly, savoring every inch of him that filled out the tailor-made suit, from his Italian designer shoes to the starched white shirt. From his perfect jaw line to his pearly white teeth, full lips and bright smile.

She sat rigidly to keep from shuddering. *Soon enough.* One day soon, he wouldn't have this effect on her. She'd be so familiar with him, she wouldn't notice how gorgeous he was. For now, she'd have to manage her response to him. How rare for her.

"Good morning, ladies," he greeted.

"Morning." Zoe gave him a quick nod and set her eyes back on the computer screen, looking at nothing in particular.

"Good morning, Mr. Blackwell," Bella said.

Ethan wagged his finger. "I told you to call me Ethan."

"Oh. Yes. Ethan. Good morning, Ethan."

"Zoe." Ethan didn't call her name in any special way, yet it still felt like he summoned her musically. "I hope you're getting all set up just fine. How about we meet up in about an hour after you've had a little more time to get settled?"

"Sure, Mr. Bl—" Zoe paused abruptly when Ethan raised his brows and tilted his head. "I mean, sure, Ethan."

"That's better. We're a team around here."

"Yes. Of course," Zoe replied.

"Good." Ethan looked at his watch. It sparkled from clear across the room. "See you in an hour."

Zoe smiled and nodded.

After another thirty minutes with Bella, she was all set up. When Bella exited her office, Zoe sat back to take things in. Eventually, she stood, walked over to check out her view overlooking the lot and beautiful landscaping of the business park.

She closed her eyes and sighed. The flutters died down, but she wondered how she'd survive working in such close proximity to this man. One way or another, she'd figure it out. She needed her job.

Four

Ethan walked into the headquarters of Blackwell Wealth Management in Lower Manhattan with positive, excited energy coursing through his veins. The first phase of their expansion plan was now complete. He, Carter and their colleague Dillon Chambers had each identified three locations to open branches in their respective territories and hired branch managers they believed were perfect fits for getting their new offices off the ground.

His mind quickly switched to Zoe and he tried, yet again, to push thoughts of her from the forefront of his mind.

Today was the day that their teams would come together for the first of their monthly management meetings at the company's main office on Wall Street. Ethan was proud of his picks for branch managers. Zoe, Jasmine and Brian all came with stellar credentials and had already begun to prove their worth.

His stride exuded the confidence he felt about being the one to come out on top of this expansion. Admittedly, it wasn't just the prospect of expansion that excited Ethan. Today he would see Zoe for the first time in a few days. With him managing several locations, he didn't get to see her on a daily basis. On the days he didn't visit her office, he thought about her often. But that was the most he could do.

As beautiful as she was, Zoe was an employee and that made her off-limits. Blackwell Wealth Management had strict rules against employee dating, and their father, William Blackwell, known to most as Bill, held his sons to an even higher standard. The company had narrowly survived sexual harassment charges from a former employee that had tainted the company's reputation for a time. They'd worked hard to overcome that past and rebuild their reputation to the point where they were recognized as one of the best places to work several years in a row now. Bill had recently graced the cover of one of the industry's most popular financial magazines because of their accomplishments and new expansion.

"Ethan."

Ethan paused just at the entrance to the conference room. "What's up?"

Carter's stride morphed into a light jog until he caught up with Ethan.

The brothers slapped hands and hugged. "You ready for me to be your boss?" Carter asked.

"Nope." Ethan shook his head. "Because that's not going to happen. This win is all mine!" Both men laughed and headed into the conference room.

A continental breakfast, coffee urns and an array of waters and juices lined the back of the room.

"Coffee?" Ethan gestured toward the food.

Carter nodded. "Looking forward to meeting your team," he said.

"Yes, I've got some great people. They're already executing. I think it's going to go well. What about yours?"

"I'm excited about what they bring to the table. We're off to a good start."

Ethan wondered briefly if he should volunteer any information about Zoe or keep his thoughts to himself.

"Ethan…" Carter called. "You with me, bro? What's on your mind?"

"Ah…nothing."

"You zoned out on me for a sec. Having reservations?"

Ethan looked at the door to the conference room to make sure no one else was coming in. "There's this one manager I hired." He lowered his voice. "Wait until you see her. Her résumé is great but to say she's a beauty is a gross understatement."

Carter's eyes widened. "And?"

"And nothing. I'm just saying she's gorgeous. I'd never do anything to jeopardize the company, but I will admit, the first couple of days weren't easy." Ethan sighed. "It took lots of concentration for me to stay focused. It's all good now but wait until you see her. You'll understand what I'm talking about. Even more than being beautiful, she's smart and she's got amazing ideas. She's probably my best pick. I can already tell that her branch will do well."

"Understood. I can't wait to see her. Beauty and brains. Perfect combination. I'm sure you're keeping your hands clean when it comes to her."

"Absolutely." Ethan waved off Carter's concern. "She's amazing to look at, but I'm a professional."

"And much more by the book than I'll ever be. Ha!" Carter laughed.

"You're right about that," Ethan agreed with a chuckle. What Carter had said was true. Since they were teens, Carter had always been a bit more rebellious. Ethan, on the other hand, avoided upsetting his father at all costs. The relationships they shared with their dad were different. Ethan had always been cautious, and for good reason.

He heard footsteps and both he and Carter looked toward the door.

Zoe stuck her head in tentatively. "Good morning, Ethan." She stepped into the room. "I was just about to ask if I was in the right place until I saw you."

"You're in the right place." Ethan turned to Carter. The two exchanged a quick, knowing look. Ethan knew Carter agreed that Zoe was as stunning as he'd claimed. He and Carter met her halfway into the room. "This is Zoe Baldwin, branch manager for the Garden City office. Zoe, this is my brother Carter Blackwell, regional director for the outer boroughs."

Carter held out his hand. "Pleasure to meet you, Zoe. Too bad you're on the losing team."

Zoe's eyes widened and she looked from Ethan to Carter.

"You wish." Ethan moved Carter out of the way. "Hungry?" he asked Zoe.

"Um." Zoe's eyes were still on Carter.

"He's a joker and unfortunately, not all that funny. Worst thing is he's also delusional, thinking that his territory has a chance of beating our numbers in the first six months. He owes me a new set of irons when he loses."

Understanding spread across Zoe's face. "Oh! I see." She laughed with Carter. "Good thing I never lose." She dropped her bag on an empty seat and headed toward the refreshments.

Carter's laughter ceased abruptly. "I like her confidence," he admitted.

When she came back with her coffee, the three of them engaged in small talk for the next several minutes until Bill, Dillon, Blackwell's executive team and the rest of their branch managers arrived. When Zoe wasn't paying attention, Carter looked at Ethan and discreetly raised his brows. He was impressed. Ethan knew they'd talk more about her later.

"Morning, morning, morning!" Bill's big voice filled the room.

Ethan stiffened at the sound of his father's booming voice, then forced himself to relax—a habit he hadn't managed to break since he was a teenager. The jovial mood had broken; it was time to get to business.

After rounds of introductions, the executive team, which included Ethan and Carter's oldest brother, Lincoln, welcomed the new branch managers and began taking them through various components of the company's strategic plan. The senior vice president of Human Resources provided them with an uplifting account of how the company's most important commodity wasn't the strength of their portfolio, but the value of their employees. The room felt energized. Everyone seemed enthusiastic about working together to meet the firm's goals.

A few incentives were offered to stir up some fun, healthy competition between the regions; for example, the office with the best numbers after the first six months would be awarded a catered breakfast and lunch sponsored by the other two offices.

Zoe looked across the table, capturing Carter's attention with a fierce, competitive gaze. With two fingers, she pointed at her own eyes and then turned those fingers around at him as if to say, *I'm watching you*.

Carter threw his head back and laughed, prompting others in the room to look around. But Zoe simply glanced at Ethan, nodded and mouthed, *We've got this*.

The meeting adjourned and everyone enjoyed a tasty catered lunch. Carter and Zoe's competitive banter painted the atmosphere colorfully, but still kept things friendly for all of the managers. By the end of lunch, the entire team had begun to bond in spite of their respective territories.

It had been a good morning for Ethan. He was excited to present his team but was most proud of the way Zoe had fit right into the Blackwell fold. He was impressed by the way she handled Carter's personality, meeting him toe-to-toe for every joke he tossed her way. Brian and Jasmine, the managers of Ethan's other locations, did well also, but of course Zoe monopolized his attention. Ethan hoped it wasn't too obvious.

The regional directors stayed behind once all the branch managers were dismissed, and Ethan and Carter went out for coffee.

Carter placed their cups of dark roast on the small bistro table at the coffee shop closest to their headquarters. "I like her."

"Who, Zoe?" Ethan asked as if Carter could have been talking about anyone else.

"No, J.Lo," Carter teased. "Of course I'm talking about Zoe."

Ethan shook his head. "Yeah" was all he said.

"She *is* gorgeous." Carter nodded slowly. "Smart, got spunk and a sense of humor. She seems like she can really hold her own."

"Yeah," Ethan said again. He realized he was smiling and sipped his coffee.

"Be careful, brother."

"What?" He reared his head back. "I can handle myself around beautiful women. I'm a professional." He had every intention of being a respectable boss. There was too much at stake otherwise.

"Mmm-hmm." Carter sipped his coffee but kept his eyes on Ethan. "Like I said, be careful."

Five

Zoe snatched her cell phone off the side table and jabbed her finger on the screen to stop the annoying chimes of her alarm. Not having the strength to put it back, she dropped the phone on the couch beside her, let her head fall against the cushion, closed her eyes and sighed. The sun had yet to rise, but if she was going to make it to work anywhere near on time, she had to get up immediately. She groaned and rubbed her neck. It hurt from sleeping in such an awkward position on the couch.

Zoe looked around the dark room and didn't see her sister Shena. She grunted, then tried to muster enough energy to get herself up off the couch.

"You're awake?"

The sound of her mother's voice startled her. Zoe watched Laura Baldwin struggle down the narrow staircase, holding the banister with both hands. Her cane dangled from under one arm.

"Hey, Ma." Zoe walked over to help her mother with the last few steps.

"Did you sleep at all?" her mother asked.

"A little."

Laura groaned. "Hardly a wink." She scanned the room. "Where is she?" she asked, referring to Shena.

"I don't know." Zoe looked around and saw that Shena's boots and sweater were no longer in the chair by the window. "She was gone when I woke up. She'll turn up," Zoe said, trying to reassure her mother. They'd been here before with Shena. She never stayed away long. Sometimes it took hours, and, unfortunately, sometimes it took a few days, but she'd always come back home.

Laura shook her head and huffed. "You have time for a little breakfast?" She started toward the kitchen.

Zoe didn't want to leave her mother, but it was too early to start taking time off from her job. She certainly didn't feel like divulging her family drama to her new boss. "I really need to get home so I can get dressed for work. Are you going in?" she asked, hoping that Laura, too, was going to work.

Being in the office would take her mother's mind off Shena instead of her sitting at home waiting by the door and the phone. Despite her mother only being in her fifties, Zoe wished she could retire early. Life hadn't been easy for them and the wear and tear showed all over her mother's body. The near-crippling car accident a few years back hadn't helped either.

"Yeah," Laura finally said after a few moments of silence. "I need to go in. Got too much to do." She paused, leaning on her walking stick with one hand on her hip. "I've tried everything. I feel so helpless." She raked her hand over her head. "I don't know what else to do."

"I know, Ma. You can't blame yourself or Shena's condition. All we can do is support her."

"If she would just stay on the medicine they give her…" Laura knit her lips together, took a deep breath and let it out with a sharp huff.

"Yeah." Zoe shrugged. "There would be fewer…" She paused trying to find the right word. She settled on "episodes" to describe Shena's hysterical state from the night before.

After days of not taking her medication, Shena seemed to have come undone and Laura had called Zoe over to help with her sister. It was their routine. Shena would take her medicine for a while, feel better and stop. Eventually, she'd have some kind of major depressive episode. They weren't sure what had sparked this current episode but believed it had something to do with recent issues with her boyfriend. It was well into the night before they'd been able to calm Shena down. But now she was gone. When she disappeared, there was no telling whether she'd return in a few hours or a few days. And Laura and Zoe would worry the entire time.

Zoe grabbed her purse and jacket from the sofa and kissed her mother. "Call me if you hear from her and I'll do the same, okay?"

"Yes. Let me know when you've made it to work."

"Okay." Zoe made it outside and tamped down her emotions. Dealing with her sister's illness was painful and exhausting. She knew that the pain she felt could never match that of her mother. That was why Zoe never hesitated to drop everything and come when called. Besides, she loved her younger sister. Caring for her was the closest she'd ever come to being a mother herself.

Zoe started the ignition but sat in the car for several moments before driving through the predawn blackness.

It seemed to serve as a metaphor for what her family was dealing with right now. Hadn't they been told it was always darkest before the dawn? Was there a dawn for her sister's condition?

Zoe headed home. Even after a shower and a light breakfast, she was still tired. She made a quick coffee stop on her way to the office. It was a café Americano kind of morning. Her regular medium roast or chai latte wasn't going to do. She ordered the largest size they had and drank as much from the steaming cup as she could by the time she pulled into the parking lot at the office. Her day felt as if it had been long already. The rest of the day would be full of meetings, including an early one with her boss, and she had to be alert.

"Morning!" Bella was especially chipper this morning.

Zoe forced a smile that she hoped matched the brightness of Bella's. "Good morning, Bella."

As she stepped farther in the office, she could tell that Ethan was already in. She'd been hoping to arrive before him to prepare for their meeting and muster up some more energy.

Zoe dipped into her office and closed the door behind her. She checked in with her mom to see if she'd heard from Shena. Of course she hadn't. After that, she gathered the résumés of the potential candidates she wanted to share with Ethan during their meeting.

There was a soft knock on her office door. Zoe cleared her throat, forced her lips into a smile and spoke through it. Feigning a cheerfulness she didn't feel in her heart, she sang, "Come in!"

"Hey!" A fresh wind seemed to accompany Ethan into her office. Like Bella, he was obviously in a great mood. Zoe held her smile. "Good morning. Did you have a good weekend?" he asked.

"Yes, I did, thanks. And you?" Zoe swallowed hard as she allowed her smile to fade.

"Great!" He sat in one of the chairs positioned in front of her desk. "Yes, me, too." He went on to describe a fun-sounding gathering he'd attended with his family to celebrate his grandfather's birthday. The details of the festivities seemed so lavish and filled with grandeur; nothing like the modest gatherings she had with her mother and sister.

Zoe pasted on her smile before she spoke. "That sounds nice."

Ethan paused, taking her in pensively. She squirmed a bit under the intensity of his gaze. It felt like she was being sized up.

"You okay?" he asked.

"Oh, yes, I'm…fine. I'm fine." Why had she said *fine* twice?

Ethan tilted his head with a measure of skepticism. "You sure?"

"Sure." She chuckled a little. "Yes, I'm sure. It sounds like you have a lovely family. A big one, too."

He analyzed her another moment before responding. "Yes. Huge. Tons of cousins on both sides." He proudly shared a bit more about his large, close-knit family.

As he spoke, Zoe pictured them all dressed elegantly in their opulent environment. The image was perfect in her mind: everyone with erect posture looking refined against the picturesque backdrop of the clubhouse he described at the golf course where they'd held the festivities.

It was all far from what she was used to. She hardly knew opulence before going away to college and working in Finance. In school, she'd met girls with more wealth than she could have ever imagined. And the financial industry had given her a taste of what that life was like through coworkers and clients. She admired it from a distance but had never craved it for herself.

Zoe was particularly proud of what she'd accomplished in her career, which afforded her a very different lifestyle than how she'd grown up. She loved her stylishly decorated yet modest townhome and was especially happy to be able to help her mother make ends meet. Occasionally, she'd treated her mom and sister to nice dinners at great restaurants and even some beach vacations over the past few years. She was responsible for her mother's very first ride on an airplane. That gave her so much joy.

"Enough about my family," Ethan said, pressing his palms flat on her desk. Zoe realized that she had tuned him out and hoped he hadn't noticed. "Well." He hauled himself up from the chair. "Ready when you are. We can meet in my office or the conference room, whichever you prefer."

"Either is fine for me."

Ethan started to walk out but turned back toward her. "And you're sure you're okay?"

"Yes. Really. Just a little tired. My weekend was…a bit exhausting. Not as fun as yours, though."

"Okay." He shrugged. "See you in about—" he looked at his watch "—ten minutes?"

"Your office?" Zoe confirmed in the most cheerful tone she could manage.

"Yes."

She watched him walk out and for once was glad to see him go. Much too soon to divulge any of her family's drama. Would there ever be a time where she'd feel comfortable speaking about that with Ethan?

She began gathering the things she needed for her meeting with Ethan when her phone rang. She was about to send it to voice mail until she saw that it was her sister's number.

"Shena!" Zoe tried not to sound frantic. Closing her office door, she lowered her voice before asking, "Where are you?"

"Home." Shena's voice was so small that it made Zoe's heart tighten. She knew her sister was in a bad way.

"Who's there with you?"

"No one. Mom went to work, I think."

Zoe sighed. "Yes. She did." Now that she knew where her sister was, she felt a little better. Shena's bipolar condition was a never-ending matter, but she was home safe for now. "I'll be there after work so we can talk, okay?"

"Yeah." Shena's voice sounded small again.

"I've got to get to work. See you later."

"Bye."

Zoe hung up feeling more like Shena's mother than her sister. She stood straight, took in a deep breath and let it out slowly before heading to Ethan's office for their meeting.

With her sister dominating her thoughts, it helped Zoe not to focus on his good looks. She didn't have to try hard to concentrate in his presence this morning. And the mention of his lavish lifestyle helped her determine that aside from work, their realities were really far apart. There wasn't much they could possibly have in common. She needed to remember that.

Six

Ethan tapped the steering wheel to the beat of an old-school R & B song on the radio. He couldn't help but smile as he made his way toward Zoe's house to pick her up.

She'd called to inform him that she'd woken up to a flat tire and would be late getting to the investment conference they were scheduled to attend in downtown Brooklyn. Immediately, Ethan had offered to pick her up along the way. He called his other two branch managers and asked if they wanted to carpool, as well, but they were already on the road. At least he'd attempted to both make Zoe feel comfortable and quiet any potential whispers about the two of them riding in together.

Ethan pulled up to her town house and texted her to let her know he'd arrived. Minutes later, she emerged from her door in a well-fitting gray skirt suit, yellow blouse and matching pumps.

He loved her sense of style. She always managed a professional yet sexy appearance with a touch of something unexpected. He hadn't seen many people pair colors the way she had, and that gray and yellow made her glow. He watched her intently until she pulled the passenger door open. He was glad he'd chosen to drive one of his sportier cars.

"Morning!" Zoe's voice rang in his ear like a melody.

"Morning." Ethan smiled and waited until she was buckled in before pulling off.

"Thanks so much for offering me a ride. I didn't want to put you out of your way, but it seemed to be the only option for me to avoid getting there late." She sighed. "At first, I was going to just change the tire but realized my rim was bent really bad. I guess that pothole I hit on my way home from my mother's house last night did more damage than I expected."

Ethan's brow furrowed when she mentioned changing the tire. He didn't want to come across as a jerk that didn't expect women to be able to do the same things as men. He thought about his words before speaking. "I like that you change tires." That was the truth. He was intrigued.

"Change tires, change oil. It takes a few major skills to be a girl these days."

"Impressive." Ethan raised a brow and trained his eyes on the road. He liked Zoe even more.

"My mom made sure of it. She wanted her girls to be okay living independently."

"Smart tree makes for a smart apple."

"Did you just call me an apple?"

"I think I did just call you an apple." The sound of their laughter filled the car. Ethan enjoyed her humor and decided he could listen to her laugh all day.

"What other interesting skills do you have?" Once the words left his lips, he realized they could seem rather suggestive.

Zoe looked over at him. He could feel the heat of her watching him.

"Okay. That didn't sound right but you have to know I had the purest of intentions," he said after several moments passed.

She grinned at him. "It's a good thing I know you're a gentleman."

"Glad my reputation preceded that comment," he said dryly.

"To answer your question, I own a great drill set, know how to shoot… What else? Oh! My sister and I spent a few years doing karate. The community center offered free classes for the youth in our neighborhood. We were the only girls. Somehow my mom found pink karate uniforms and insisted that our instructor allow us to wear them."

"Wow. So you can fight, shoot and fix cars? If I had a type I think that would be it—a pink-gi-wearing, karate-fighting, gun-toting, car-fixing, hole-drilling apple."

Zoe laughed hard. Ethan imagined that if beauty had a sound, her laugh would be it.

"Where did you learn to shoot?"

"My uncle lived deep in the country down in South Carolina. He hunted, and taught us when my sister and I went down during the summer. What about you? What are your special skills?"

Zoe's question sounded as suggestive as his had. Ethan swallowed before responding. His mind veered into naughty territory and he had to rein his thoughts in. Though he couldn't act on it, he couldn't deny her effect on him.

He finally answered, "I collect cars. It's one of my hobbies. My parents said I've been obsessed with them since I was a kid. You know those little Matchbox cars and Hot Wheels? Yeah, I had hundreds of them growing up. Every birthday, every Christmas, all I asked for was more cars. I had special cases for them and everything. My mom said that by the time I was three, I was calling out the makes and models on the cars that passed us on the highway. I even memorized license plate numbers."

"Seriously! Wow. How many cars do you own?"

"Five."

Zoe's eyes bulged. "Five? What kinds? Makes and models!" she added.

"This one," he said, referencing the top-of-the-line BMW coupe they rode in. "My convertible is an Aston Martin, the Bentley is an SUV, the Silverado is my pickup." Ethan noticed Zoe nod knowingly as she counted on her fingers. "Then there's my favorite baby, the coal-black 1969 Mustang." He was sure his pride was evident as he described his last vehicle.

"No kidding? Mustangs are my favorite. 1969? Ah! That must be a beauty."

"You like old cars?"

"Love them! You restored it yourself?"

Ethan would have driven the Mustang had he known she would have loved that one. But he often reserved that for special drives. "Yep. But I probably spend more time cleaning it than driving it. I only take her out on special occasions."

"Okay. What else?" she asked. Her voice was melodic.

"What else what?" Ethan asked.

"What else don't I know about you?"

Zoe obviously didn't know her effect on him but he

couldn't possibly say that. "I did a little karate when I was a kid, too. Nothing major. My dad, brothers and I are big golfers. Other than that, you can say I'm pretty adventurous."

"Oh? What kinds of adventures?"

"Anything that gets the adrenaline flowing and makes the heart pump a little faster. You know, like fast cars and things like skydiving and four-wheeling."

Zoe smiled. "Skydiving and four-wheeling sounds like fun. The height of my adrenaline-rush ventures would probably include the big roller coasters at Six Flags. Oh, I did go zip-lining once. That made my stomach do flips but I liked it." She chuckled and shook her head.

Ethan was enjoying their conversation. He wanted to hear more. Communicating had come easy for the two of them from the start. He hadn't expected that ease to transfer into playful banter but was glad it had. For once, he wasn't annoyed at the dense rush-hour traffic crawling across the Belt Parkway. He could have stayed in the car laughing and getting to know Zoe all day.

The more she talked about herself, the more intrigued he became. They talked about everything from their backgrounds to work to dreams to politics. Zoe had strong opinions on the latter. They debated current events and shared their favorite shows to binge watch. Ethan was a fan of older shows like *Law & Order* and *Criminal Minds*. Zoe could tolerate those but was a bigger fan of newer series like the ones on Netflix.

It took well over an hour and a half to reach the hotel where the conference was being held. Had it not been for the heavy traffic, they could have made it there in a half hour. New York had its own brand of rush hour painted with impatience, colorful language from angry drivers, aggressive maneuvers and obnoxious horn blowing. Despite the long drive, Ethan felt like they'd arrived too soon. His time of having Zoe all to himself was over. Suddenly he looked forward to the evening drive. Traffic would be just as bad, if not worse, but having Zoe in the car with him would make it all worthwhile.

By the time they arrived, they'd bonded. Ethan couldn't lie. He liked Zoe—a lot. She was incredibly sexy, and he was definitely attracted to her. But she was his employee, which made her off-limits. The most they could be was good friends.

He wished he had met her under different circumstances. Everything about her was refreshing—her conversation, wit, intelligence, style—everything. And the fact that she could change a tire and loved Mustangs gave her bonus points. He hadn't met a woman quite like her before.

There was an undercurrent of strength, resilience and grit about Zoe that he found captivating. That had been missing in the women he'd dated before. Ethan hadn't known how attractive those qualities were until now.

He maneuvered the car into the parking garage under the hotel where the conference was being held. There was a lot more to Zoe than what met the eye. It was all nicely arranged in a beautiful, smart, feminine package. He would have to exercise some special restraint to focus throughout this conference. His curiosity had been seriously piqued.

Once the car was handed over to a valet, they headed for the elevator. Reaching for the call button at the same time, their hands brushed one another's. Both paused and smiled awkwardly.

Something electrifying generated from the area her hand had touched and traveled up the length of his entire arm. Ethan swallowed hard and cleared his throat. He knew he hadn't imagined that feeling and wondered if Zoe felt the same thing.

It was going to be a long day.

Seven

As Zoe and Ethan approached the registration table inside the luxury hotel, she tried to shake off the heat that still lingered from being so close to him during their car ride. And that car of his... She'd never been inside a vehicle with that magnitude of luxury. She'd been super proud of her sporty Acura. It was an upgrade for her and had all the premium features. But Ethan's BMW was made for driving.

She loved cars. Despite the potholes that New Yorkers knew all too well, their ride today had been extremely smooth. At times she could have been convinced that the vehicle hadn't actually touched the road. The seats had enveloped her in soft leather. The music had filled the interior with a crispness that had made her feel like the singers could have been sitting in the back seat.

Reflecting on their conversation, Zoe didn't know why she felt so comfortable chatting it up with Ethan. He was so easy to talk to—and fun. She enjoyed his sense of humor, and the way he tapped into hers carried their jokes even further.

They checked in, received their badges and were directed to the great ballroom for breakfast before the conference started. Ethan led them to a table with a sign that displayed their company name. She looked up and smiled when she saw the Blackwell Wealth Management logo flash across the large screens flanking the small stage and podium. She was proud that Blackwell had been one of the sponsors at the conference.

Zoe found a seat and put down her bag. She spotted Jasmine, waved and pointed toward their reserved table. She looked around for Ethan, but he seemed to have disappeared.

The room buzzed with energy. Well-dressed finance professionals from all across the metropolitan area were in attendance. Zoe spotted a few familiar faces as she made her way toward the buffet. She hadn't made many friends in the industry, so she didn't go out of her way to say hello to anyone she recognized. She'd greet them once they were in closer proximity. Her old boss, Seth, popped into her mind and she hope she didn't see him. She stepped into the buffet line and picked up a plate.

"Look who we have here."

At the sound of Seth's voice, all the warmth she'd settled into on her ride to the conference dissipated instantly. Zoe closed her eyes, held her plate with both hands and breathed deeply. She wished she hadn't thought of him and blamed herself for conjuring up his presence. Slowly, she turned around. He was immediately behind her in line. Way too close for her liking.

"Seth." She nodded coolly.

"How's the new gig?" His eyes washed over her from head to toe.

"Great. It's great." She offered a tight smile and turned to focus on the eggs and bacon she put on her plate.

"Glad to hear it."

Zoe decided to choose her selections quickly so she could get back to her table and as far from Seth as possible. "Good seeing you," she lied evenly.

"Yeah. It's good seeing you, too." He stepped uncomfortably close to her. His tone made her look his way. A sly smile eased across his face. Was he trying to flirt with her or intimidate her? "Tell me, did you file that complaint because you didn't get the promotion?"

Zoe just blinked a few times before narrowing her eyes at him. Anger crept up her spine. She filed the complaint because of his inappropriate behavior but it wasn't taken seriously. Seth's behavior persisted. After getting passed over for the second promotion she knew that leaving the company would be inevitable.

Seth reared his head back and dismissed her concern with a wave. "I'm not mad. You were upset. I get it." He stepped in even closer, eliminating any space between them. Zoe stepped back. He smirked. "Maybe if you had been a bit more—" he seemed to search for a word "—friendlier with me, one of those promotions could have been yours."

She gritted her teeth, whipped around and walked away. It was the best she could do without causing a scene.

"We should have lunch one day," he said to her retreating back. She kept walking.

She marched back to the table with steam rising inside of her. She saw that more of the Blackwell team had arrived and she willed herself to calm down. She greeted Bill and Carter, who were standing nearby holding court with Ethan and a few others from Blackwell's headquarters. They greeted her warmly.

She could have sworn she saw Carter pass Ethan a quick look. She couldn't read it but wondered what was behind it. Did it have something to do with her? She shook off that thought. They were brothers. It could have been anything.

Zoe headed to the Blackwell table and took her seat. She began to dig into her breakfast but found she'd lost her appetite.

"I'm not sure if you heard me," Seth said, startling her. She hadn't realized that he had walked up behind her. "I'd like to do…lunch sometime soon. I hope you're not harboring any hard feelings about, you know, from our work together."

This guy was unbelievable. Zoe pulled in her bottom lip before rising slowly. "Seth." She wanted to tell him to leave her alone but chose other words instead. "No." She forced a smile. "No hard feelings. In fact, I should thank you. Standing in the way of me getting ahead actually helped me to spread my wings. Now I have a dream job with amazing people, making so much more money. So don't worry. I'm doing just fine. And no, I don't think we should do lunch. Thank you!" She tilted her head and gave him a satisfied smile.

Seth opened his mouth but didn't speak. He recovered quickly. "Fine. That's great."

She folded her arms and tilted her head, almost daring him to say more.

"Well. How about instead of lunch, dinner would be even better?" He lowered his voice. "I've always been attracted to—" he quickly looked around, then drew closer, forcing her to move back "—women like you."

Zoe's eyebrows furrowed. "Women like me?"

Seth's slick smile returned. "Yeah. You know, from the other side of the fence, the tracks, whatever. You women of color got sass and I like it. What do you say? We don't work together anymore. It can't hurt."

Zoe felt like her temperature had risen by ten degrees in that singular moment. She pointed her finger close to his nose and opened her mouth to douse him with some of the sass he liked so much.

"Ethan Blackwell, of Blackwell Wealth Management." Ethan broke into that moment like a whip. He held his hand out to Seth. "And you are?" He carefully placed his hand on Zoe's lower back.

Zoe closed her mouth, thankful for his sharp interruption. How had he known she needed someone to step in at just that time?

For a brief second, Seth just looked at him. "Ah. Seth Sanders." He took his eyes off Ethan for a moment, looked at Zoe, then back at Ethan. "Um. Good to meet you." He didn't bother to say what company he worked for. "See you around, Zoe." His departure was swift.

Zoe huffed, crossed her arms again and shook her head.

"Old boyfriend?"

"Ugh! No. Former jerk of a boss from my last job. Part of the reason I left."

"Lucky me. I should have thanked him instead of running him off. Does he know what he lost?" Ethan picked up one of the water glasses on the table and sipped it.

Zoe let her arms drop to her sides. "I doubt it. It's hard for him to see around his own ego."

"Oh. One of those. You okay now?"

"Thanks for bailing me out of that."

"You looked like you were about to blow. Between the pursed lips and the finger you almost poked his eye out with, I knew he wasn't a welcome guest. I hope I wasn't being too forward by placing my hand on your back. I wasn't trying to be inappropriate. I just wanted to help."

"No. I'm fine, and thanks again."

"Anytime."

He picked up another glass of ice water and handed it to Zoe. "It's the strongest drink I can muster at this time of the morning."

That made her smile. "Thanks." She took the glass and drank. It helped cool her down. Ethan didn't know it but coming to her rescue in the smooth way he had scored with her in a big way. She could still feel the imprint of his hand where he'd touched her back. It tingled deliciously.

An older gentleman with perfectly cropped gray hair, stark blue eyes, a strong jaw and perfect posture took to the podium in what Zoe determined to be an expensive blue custom-made suit. Turned out, he was the CEO of one of the largest global investment banking firms and on the boards of some major companies, according to his bio inside the conference pamphlet. He was a true Wall Street man who looked every bit of the part.

The gentleman welcomed the conference attendees, thanked the sponsors and delivered a brief state-of-the-industry address. After his speech, he announced that everyone should head to their breakout sessions.

Zoe's schedule included two full days of sessions, meetings, lunches, a dinner and a highly anticipated closing reception at the end of the second day. She wondered if she would be able to ride with Ethan again the next day since their team hadn't bothered booking a room at the host hotel. She wouldn't have time to take care of her bent rim and flat tire until after the conference. Missing any part of the conference was the last thing she wanted; this was the first time in her career that she'd been in a position high enough to participate in these kinds of events.

Zoe followed the rest of her team out of the ballroom to her first session, which was led by a Robert Richford, the CEO of a company providing similar services as Blackwell.

Zoe headed toward the door as the session came to a close. She wanted to compliment the presenter for how much she'd learned but by the time she got to the front of the room, he'd been flanked by people waiting to speak with him. She waited, assuming he'd be a great person to connect with and follow.

When she reached the front of the line, she held out her hand to Robert. "Zoe Baldwin," she said.

"You're part of the Blackwell team, right?" he asked.

"Yes," she said, smiling.

"I thought so. I saw you with them earlier. I hear they're expanding," Robert continued, friendly and interested.

"Yes. I manage one of the Long Island branches."

"Oh really? That's great. Who's your regional director?"

"Ethan Blackwell."

"Right. Yes. Well, here's my card." Robert handed Zoe a card from a designer case. "Perhaps we should have coffee sometime soon. Talk shop. Do some good old-fashioned networking. I promise I won't try to steal you from Blackwell." He chuckled.

"That would be amazing," she said enthusiastically. "I know you must be a busy man. Let me know your schedule and I'll work mine around it."

"Will do." He smiled, nodded and addressed the next person in line.

There was something oddly familiar about Robert, now that she'd spoken with him up close. Zoe wondered what had made him suggest coffee with her specifically, yet she was happy that he had. Willena had always told her that networking was important. Zoe needed to do it more often.

She continued to the next session where Blackwell was slated for a presentation on managing change. The panel was led by the senior Mr. Blackwell, along with Carter, Dillon and Ethan.

Zoe and her team watched intently as the three of them shared their knowledge of market trends and the best ways to navigate the ever-changing environment of the industry. She was especially impressed with Ethan's savvy style of communication. Both he and Carter were witty and elicited a few chuckles from the audience, but Ethan had a certain charm that really pulled people in. As she listened to all of them, her chest swelled with pride for simply being part of the Blackwell team, but she did have one burning question.

Zoe raised her hand. Ethan looked her way. She could have sworn she saw him attempting to hide a smile. She locked eyes with him briefly.

"My question is with regards to diversity, specifically when it comes to women. While I truly believe each and every one of you are brilliant and appreciate the knowledge you have shared, looking at your all-male panel does raise the concern about how our industry looks when it comes to opportunities for women at the top.

Can you tell me what changes you see with the roles of women in this industry?"

Several women in the audience applauded her question.

Zoe looked directly at Ethan, and that smile he'd seemed to be hiding eased across his lips.

"I'd love to answer that." Bill raised his index finger.

"Thank you, Mr. Blackwell."

Bill went on to answer Zoe's question in the most favorable way, first speaking to the fact that despite what the presentation of the panelists may suggest, Blackwell's ratio of men to women was just about fifty percent. He further explained some of the major changes across the industry to ensure that they were operating in the most equitable fashion and spoke of the value and expertise that the women on his team brought to the firm.

"Speaking of which, Ms. Baldwin, I think you should join us up here the next time we lead a panel. We can truly show the value that the women and men of Blackwell bring."

"I'd like that, Mr. Blackwell. Thank you for answering my question."

"I'd like to echo my father's comments," Ethan began, "and add that we've worked hard to ensure that we're pulling the best possible talent from the most diverse pool possible. It takes all perspectives to ensure that a company can truly meet the needs of clients and thrive. Diversity shouldn't be an item on an organization's list to check off. It should be imbedded in the DNA of the organization because it impacts every area of a successful business, especially the bottom line."

A proud smile spread across Zoe's face this time. Blackwell was so unlike her last company. She glanced around to see if Seth was in the room. He wasn't, and she actually wished he had been to hear what Ethan had just said. Once again, Ethan scored more points with her. Not that she was counting.

Once the panel ended, people flooded the front of the room to speak with Dillon and the Blackwell men. *The Blackwell men.* They must have made Mrs. Blackwell and the rest of their huge family so proud. Based on Zoe's conversations with Ethan, family seemed to be everything to him. She was sure they had their issues, but on the surface, they appeared to be a perfect bunch.

She intentionally hadn't mentioned much at all about her sister and mother during the family-centered parts of their conversation during the car ride to the conference.

Zoe looked toward the front of the room. Lots of attendees still milled about, speaking to the Blackwell men. She took notice of the posture of some of the women as they addressed Carter, Dillon and especially Ethan. Some of their body language was a bit flirtatious. A twinge of jealousy hit her and she literally shook her head in an attempt to shake it off. She had no reason to be jealous of the attention women lavished on Ethan.

Zoe pulled out her schedule, checked in with her fellow branch managers and headed off to her next session. As much as she convinced herself how crazy it was to feel jealous, she wasn't interested in standing around watching women pine over Ethan. She walked out of the room, wondering how many of them suggested "lunch or dinner" with him.

She acknowledged to herself that she was being ridiculous. Ethan was nothing more than her boss. That was all he would ever be.

Eight

"I heard you boys did a good job on the panel at the conference the other day," Ethan's mom, Lydia, said as she sat gracefully at the end of the large dining table. A feast fit for a king's court was spread before them.

She had baked a ham and made stuffed fish, basmati rice infused with fresh herbs, and roasted green beans. Since their children had become adults, Bill had been trying to encourage her to allow someone else to cook for them, but she enjoyed it too much to put it in someone else's hands—especially when it came to cooking for her family.

Bill sat on the opposite end of the table. Between them, their son Lincoln, his wife, Britney, and their two young children, Ava and Logan, occupied one side while Ethan, Carter and their younger sister, Ivy, sat on the other. Even though Ivy was just two years younger than

Ethan, they still emphasized the word *little* when they spoke of their younger sister.

Carter had invited his woman of the month—a curvy lawyer named Edison Wells, with honey-colored hair and skin the color of a blanched almond. To everyone else's surprise, this was the second family dinner that Edison had attended.

Today was one of their family Sunday dinners. Once their children had graduated from college and become adults, Bill and Lydia had declared a family day rather than see less of them. Despite their schedules, the entire family came together for dinner on the first Sunday of every month. Until now, Carter had never brought the same "friend" to dinner twice. Everyone around the table was especially tickled.

"Who mentioned that? Was it Dad?" Carter teased his mother regarding her comment about them doing well at the conference. "I'm glad you told us, Ma. Otherwise we may have never known." He chuckled. "You know Dad isn't one to dole out too much praise."

Bill was known for being stern and didn't shell out compliments often, lest his boys become complacent. He was different with his daughter, Ivy. He complimented her and his lovely wife every chance he got.

"Yeah," Lincoln added. "Dad can be stingy with the accolades."

Each sibling laughed except Ethan. He simply placed a forkful of his mother's delicious salmon in his mouth. Bill's lack of acknowledgment was something for his brothers to tease their dad about on a regular basis. It touched Ethan differently. For him, the subject wasn't so light. Ethan wanted his dad's approval. He wasn't needy at all, but his father's affirmation was extremely important to him.

"Okay, okay." Bill wiped his mouth with a cloth napkin. "Let's not make this Tease Bill Sunday. You're all doing a wonderful job. Okay. Is that better?"

"Bill!" Lydia admonished. She turned to her sons with a smile. "You know your father means well. He's just set in his ways and wants you to continue to reach high. Right, Bill?"

Bill playfully lifted a brow. "Could be."

Lincoln and Carter teased their father a bit more, and he dismissively waved his hand at their banter. Light laughter flitted around the table. Ethan still hadn't joined in any of the jokes.

"Yeah, but it would be nice to hear something affirming from you every now and then." Ethan's expression was stoic. His tone even.

The laughter subsided. Lydia sighed. Bill cleared his throat and the other siblings said nothing.

"Dad. It's just good to know when we have the big man's approval," Lincoln added in what appeared to be an attempt to break the thickening silence.

"I see." Bill's tone was flat.

"Okay, family. It's time for dessert. I made a pecan pie," Lydia announced. She stood and clasped her hands together.

"Yes! I guess I'll have to run that extra mile tomorrow morning," Ivy said. "I'm having a piece of this pie."

"I get the first slice. I'm the oldest." Lincoln raised his hand.

"I'm the youngest," Ivy challenged.

"No!" Logan, Lincoln's son, wagged his little finger. "Ava's the youngest." He pointed to his four-year-old sister and then jabbed his own chest. "And then me!" he said and giggled.

Laughter rose around the table again.

"He has a point," Britney said. "And since I'm their mom and I have to feed them, I should get my piece first along with them."

"Yeah, right!" Carter called out.

"Ha! Nice try, Brit," Ivy said.

"Didn't work, huh?" Britney shrugged and grinned.

Ethan laughed that time but was still a bit affected by the jokes around Bill withholding praise from his boys. He understood his father, but his way never sat well with Ethan. Then again, his situation with his father was different.

"Dessert is served," Lydia announced, placing the pie on the table.

"You only made one!" Ivy frowned. "What're the rest of them going to have?"

"Girl! I don't know where you put all this food." Lydia plopped back into her seat and sniffed. "Metabolism must be on one thousand."

"Yeah. She burns a lot of calories running—" Carter paused for effect "—her mouth!" He looked at his niece and nephew with a cheesy smile, then threw his head back and howled. The two children snickered.

Ivy tossed a napkin at him. "If that's the case, you should be the smallest person in the room but then again—" she turned to the kids "—how would his body hold up that huge head of his?"

Ava and Logan covered their mouths with their little hands and giggled harder.

Ivy winked at them and blew an air kiss to her brother. Carter acted as if he caught it. "Which one of you want this kiss from auntie?" he asked.

"Meeee!" both kids yelled, raising their hands.

"Ivy, we need another one," Carter said.

She kissed her hand and together she and Carter

tossed the imaginary kisses at the kids, who pretended to catch them and slap them on their cheeks. The sweet moment elicited more than a few *aww*s.

Together, the family dug into the pecan pie. Moans of pleasure rolled around the table as they ate. Once dessert was finished, everyone helped clear the table. The women took to the sitting room and the men headed toward the sliding doors to go onto the deck for their usual after-dinner boy talk.

Bill slowed, gently tugging Ethan's arm. Ethan turned and looked into his father's face. Bill looked pensive.

"What's up, Pop?"

Bill looked around Ethan to make sure his other sons had made it out onto the deck. "I've been meaning to speak to you about something. Come."

Ethan followed his father into the study.

"I noticed how you touched Zoe's back at the conference the other day," Bill began. "The gesture seemed rather…familiar."

Ethan shifted on his feet. He'd only thought about the possible implications of placing his hand on Zoe's back after it was done. His intention had just been to rescue Zoe from a guy who was making her uncomfortable. He cleared his throat and continued to listen.

"You're not involved with this woman, are you?" Bill's eyes narrowed.

"No!" Ethan said quickly. "No, Dad."

Bill sighed. "I don't have to remind you about the situation we dealt with before."

"No, Dad, I wouldn't put our company in jeopardy."

Bill looked disappointed. That bothered Ethan.

"It took a long time for us to overcome that situation. We have to continue to do the right thing by our employees." Bill raised his hands. "If you're involved with her in any way, it needs to stop immediately. If you're not, you have to be careful that your familiarity with this woman isn't misconstrued as any kind of inappropriate behavior."

Ethan felt a heavy sigh coming. He held his breath, not wanting to appear exasperated. He understood Bill's concern, and Ethan's feelings for Zoe made all of this much more complicated.

That sexual harassment claim had almost ruined Blackwell's reputation. Five years before, one of the male managers made a joke in poor judgment and a number of inappropriate comments that made several female team members uncomfortable. One brave woman filed a claim. The management at Blackwell responded immediately, launching an investigation, holding forums and ensuring that employees understood the company's strong stance against harassment. In the end the man apologized to all the women at the firm and was let go. However, due to the media exposure, the incident still caused a stain on the financial giant. It took a few years to clear their name.

"We're in the middle of a very critical expansion," Bill continued. "A problem like this could ruin everything. There's too much at stake here, our growth, our reputation, the culture we've worked so hard to rebuild." He placed a hand on Ethan's shoulder. "And possibly your chances at a promotion, son."

That last comment felt like a punch to Ethan's gut.

"I trust that you're capable of making good decisions. I can trust you in this, right?" Bill looked directly into Ethan's eyes.

Ethan swallowed. Of course he didn't intend to cause any problems. "Yes, Dad. Of course you can trust me."

Bill patted Ethan's shoulder and nodded. "Good." The

two men stood facing one another for several moments. Finally, Bill sighed and nodded. "Good," he said, as if he had more to say but had settled on repeating himself. "Let's go outside."

Ethan followed him through the sliding doors onto the deck for their usual conversation, cigars and scotch. Bill sparked the stone firepit to take the slight autumn chill out of the air.

It took a while for Ethan's tight disposition from their conversation to dissipate. After a while, he loosened up enough to enjoy sitting with his dad and brothers, talking about everything and nothing all the same. Sharp opinions on who would make it to the bowl game clashed. Ethan and Carter talked about how well their office expansions were doing and teased each other about what they would ask for when the other brother lost their personal bet.

When the sun had fully descended with a spectacular show of colors, Bill headed inside to watch TV with the ladies. Lincoln said his goodbyes, noting the need for him and Britney to get the kids home and into bed, leaving Ethan and Carter out on the porch, alone.

"You okay, bro?"

Carter's question caught Ethan off guard. "Me? Yeah. I'm fine."

Silence settled between them as they sipped from their glasses and puffed their cigars.

"If I tell you something," Carter said at last, "you have to promise to keep it to yourself."

Ethan looked at his brother with concern. "Of course. What's up?"

Carter took in a deep breath. "I don't know if I want to stay with the company."

Ethan's eyes widened. "I'm assuming you haven't said anything to Dad about this."

"Nope! You saw how unhappy he was when Lincoln decided to leave to do his own thing."

"Yes. He dreams of having his sons take over the business. What is it that you want to do instead?"

"I don't know. Just something different. I don't plan on leaving yet. I just know this is not what I want to do forever. It's been on my mind a lot lately."

The quiet of the night took over once again. After a while, Carter continued. "I don't know. Maybe it's a phase." He paused again. "Me wanting to leave doesn't mean I don't plan on beating you in this challenge," he said after a while.

"Aw. Your confidence is admirable." Ethan patted Carter's shoulder. "I hope you don't feel too bad when you lose." Both men laughed. Ethan needed that laugh.

"Anyway," Carter interrupted. "How are you doing?" He shifted in his chair and put his foot up on the ottoman. "I noticed you seemed a bit tight during dinner and when you and Dad finally came out onto the deck. You always get a little…you know…quiet when we talk about some of Dad's ways. Why does it bother you so much?"

Ethan was always ready for a good round of jokes but had never liked that his father didn't believe it was necessary to share his approval of his boys. He understood Bill's sternness and he loved his parents immensely, but he also knew something about them that his siblings didn't. He'd been warned never to tell a soul. Ethan and his siblings were close, and they had always shared everything—except this one secret. And it was because of this secret that Ethan desired Bill's approval the most.

"I don't know, man," he finally responded. "It's just important to me, I guess. It's hard for me to make light of."

"It's important to me, too, but despite that, we know how proud he is of us whether he says it or not."

"Of course. But it would still be nice to hear that directly from him."

"True." Carter nodded and sipped his scotch.

"Let's get to the subject on the forefront of everyone's mind." A Cheshire grin spread across Ethan's face. He looked back at the door to make sure no one was approaching. "So Edison made it to a second family dinner. Is she on her way to being my new sister-in-law?"

"Whoa, whoa. Been there… Well, almost," Carter said of the wedding that hadn't actually happened. "Not sure about going back. Edison and I are friends just having a good time. That's all."

"Cool. Just enjoying each other's company, huh?"

"Till the wheels blow off."

Ethan chuckled. "Uh-huh." Since the disastrous end to Carter's engagement a few years ago, he'd taken to running from love like he was being chased by a wild animal. He hadn't dated seriously in years and it wasn't due to a lack of options. However, it was nice to see him enjoying one woman's company even if it was short-lived.

Their conversation reminded Ethan about Zoe. He enjoyed her company a lot, too. He knew he shouldn't but Ethan wished for more time like that with her. The conversation never dulled. Even their periods of silence were comfortable. He cleared his throat. She penetrated his thoughts way too often. Maybe he needed to find someone else's company to enjoy so he could take his focus off Zoe. He couldn't be with her anyway.

He leaned toward Carter as if he had a grand secret to tell and asked, "Does your friend have a friend?"

"Ha! She has plenty of friends, but you wouldn't be interested."

Ethan reared his head back. "Why wouldn't I?"

Carter tossed him a skeptical stare.

Ethan held his hands up. "What?"

"One word… Zoe."

Ethan looked back at the door again. "What? Zoe! She's my employee," he said incredulously.

"And that doesn't seem to stop you from being sweet on her."

"Wh-what?" he stammered.

"You can fake it with your team, but I know you too well, brother. You've been sweet on her since the day she stepped into your office for her first interview. Not that you've done anything wrong," Carter assured him. "And before you ask, no, there aren't any rumors sliding around that I know of. I just know you. I see it as clear as a sunny day. It's in your eyes when you speak about her. The way you smile at the mention of her name. It's evident in the way you try to avoid her when everyone is around. You can fool them, boy, but you can't fool me."

Ethan closed his gaping mouth. There was nothing to say. He was close to all his siblings, but the tie between him and Carter was even more unbreakable. Now his father was suspicious, too. He thought back to their earlier conversation. Bill was right. There was too much at stake. Aside from his possible promotion, Ethan would hate to be the cause of something terrible happening to Blackwell's reputation at such a critical time. He needed to be more careful around Zoe.

"Yet she's untouchable," he said.

"It doesn't help that she's gorgeous." Carter smirked, looked out over the massive yard and took another sip of his drink.

Ethan chuckled before taking a sip of his own scotch. He sighed. What more could he say? Zoe was working her way into his system beyond his control. And she was totally off-limits.

Nine

Zoe loved the city, but the energy and excitement of Manhattan came at a cost. After navigating the thick rush-hour crowds on the Long Island Rail Road and subway system for this month's management meeting, she was glad she no longer had to deal with that commute on a daily basis.

The weather reports predicted a storm would roll through the city late that evening, but strong winds had already begun to kick up. Wall Street ended abruptly at the Hudson River, and that coupled with the high winds added an unseasonable chill to the air.

Zoe held her coat tight at the neck. The wind beat her face and blew fiercely through her hair, giving her more to contend with as she pushed her way through downtown streets toward the headquarters for Blackwell Wealth Management. It was too early for scarves and gloves, but she wished she had put both on before leaving the house. If the winds were any stronger, she imagined they would pick her up and set her down a few yards back.

Their monthly management meetings usually lasted a full day, but Bill had already mentioned they were likely to end the meeting early to allow everyone to get home safely before the hurricane they'd been tracking would hit their area. Zoe had stocked her and her mother's refrigerators with anything and everything they could possibly need to ride out the storm. She looked forward to a cozy night and full weekend of wine, pajamas, movies and snacks.

She was glad her sister's health was stabilized. When she'd gone to speak with Shena at their mother's house that one night, she'd convinced Shena to get back on her medicine. Shena agreed and had been doing well since. Hopefully it would last. Maybe Zoe would even have Shena join her, or she'd go to her mother's house and spend her movie-watching, pajama-wearing weekend with them. The day was just starting. She had plenty of time to decide.

Braving the increasing winds, Zoe made it into the office fifteen minutes early. She checked in with Security and headed up the twenty flights to Blackwell's offices.

Some of the team had already arrived. Her colleagues stood around the conference room in clusters of two and three, gnawing on fruit and bagels. The smell of fresh-brewed coffee scented the air, and her stomach growled.

"Stand down!" She swatted her belly playfully before placing her coat and bag in a seat next to her fellow branch manager, Jasmine.

Jasmine stopped chewing and chuckled into her hand.

"I felt the same way," she said. "I was starving by the time I got here."

"I actually had a fistfight with the wind," Zoe joked. She gestured at her windblown hair. "Obviously I lost."

"Ha!" Jasmine laughed. "It still looks better than mine." She pointed to her own head. It wasn't bad, but it wasn't the perfectly coiffed style she normally wore.

"Be right back." Zoe spun around and headed to the bathroom to assess the damage done to her hair. She finger-combed some of it back into place, freshened her lipstick and washed her hands before returning to the conference room.

She headed to the array of pastries on the console in the back of the conference room. Choosing a sesame bagel, she dug out the bready center and filled it with cream cheese. Then she made herself a steaming cup of coffee and flavored it with a creamer. She took a long, slow sniff. The French vanilla creamer made her mouth water.

After a bite and a sip, she moaned. "Jazz," she began, shortening Jasmine's name, "either this is the best darn bagel and coffee I've ever had or I'm hungry as *heck*!"

"I promise you're hungry as heck, but enjoy nonetheless," Jasmine said.

The women laughed just as Ethan and Carter walked through the doors. Zoe sat a little straighter, noting the impact of his presence on her every single time. She would sit straighter, smile harder, smooth her hair into place even if it wasn't mussed. She'd check her teeth for lipstick stains. His presence kept her on guard whether she admitted it or not. She just hoped no one else noticed. Quickly, she tried to eject a sesame seed that had lodged its way into the small gap between her two front teeth before speaking.

"Morning!" Carter sang.

"Good morning, everyone." Ethan's deep voice rolled through her like electrified molasses. It was sweet but still made her tingle.

Morning greetings sprang out across the room.

"Some wind out there, huh?" he acknowledged as he pulled off his overcoat and sat directly across from Zoe.

She would have preferred for him to sit next to her. It would have been easier not to have to look into his gorgeous face. Now she'd have to actively avoid looking at him. She had also caught him staring on several occasions.

Moments later, everyone else had arrived and settled into their seats with various combinations of breakfast foods on paper plates. Bill walked into the room, snatching all the attention. He was a distinguished-looking gentleman who carried himself with perfect posture. His stature exuded importance yet was still warm. Ethan was just like his father.

"Good morning, all, let's dig right in. We'll try to get you all out of here as soon as possible so you can go on home and get comfortable before this big storm sweeps in tonight. Dillon, let's start with your territory."

"Certainly, Bill." Dillon's team stood and made their way to the front of the room to report on their progress.

Carter's team went next and the reporting was rounded out by Ethan's. Carter led in number of new clients, but Ethan's team was in the lead with the amount of assets acquired. Dillon was close behind on both.

There was so much to go over. Despite how swiftly they moved from one subject to another, the hours rolled on, and before they knew it, it was time for lunch. They jumped right into the next topics after lunch and planned to shorten some of the reports and presentations to let everyone start on their way home.

Suddenly, Bill's executive assistant, Monica, ran into the room to tell the team what was happening outside. At twenty stories off the ground in a sturdy steel-reinforced skyscraper, they were cushioned from the true impact of the elements. All they saw were gray skies and rain.

Bill switched one of the several flat screens from its usual financial channel to the breaking news Monica had told the group about. Everyone balked at what they saw.

The storm was hitting earlier, harder and faster than anyone had expected. Strong winds had already knocked out power lines in areas right outside and around the city. Several trains in the subway system were affected by the outages and were now dealing with signal problems. Large debris had been blown across the rails for some of the commuter trains. Zoe hoped she could get out of the city without any major delays.

Bill called the meeting to a close and told everyone to make their way home as best they could and to check in once they arrived. The group said quick goodbyes and headed out.

Jasmine, Brian, Zoe and Ethan, who were all headed to Long Island, agreed to travel to Penn Station together. Less than twenty minutes later, they arrived to find the station in a state of complete chaos, teeming with people waiting on trains and complaining of delays and cancellations. They navigated through the dense crowd as closely as possible, trying to find information on when their trains would depart to Long Island.

Jasmine found that her train was leaving in seven minutes. She hugged her coworkers and raced through the throngs of people toward her platform. Brian decided to head to his mother's house in Queens and jumped on a subway that was still operating. That left Ethan and Zoe to wait on information about their trains.

Zoe dialed Jasmine to make sure she'd boarded safely.

"I made it, but you won't believe how many people are on this train," Jasmine said breathlessly. "I'm squished against the door. A lot of folks couldn't get on and have to wait for the next one. What time is your train leaving?"

"Lucky you. I don't know what time my train will leave. They pushed the departure back. They keep changing the information. The signaling problems seem to be affecting more and more lines. Let me know when you get home, okay?"

"And you do the same," Jasmine replied.

"Look at this." Ethan held his phone out so Zoe could see what he was watching. He handed her one of his earbuds so she could hear over the noise in the station.

She watched and listened in awe as a weather situation like none she'd ever seen in all her days as a New Yorker played out before her. This was worse than the superstorm the city had experienced several years before.

Breaking news announced that the storm had in fact hit the tristate area well in advance of when they'd anticipated, bringing with it harsh elements and extreme winds. It had already dumped several inches of rain across New Jersey and was dumping just as much over New York City. It swept across the city with a swift vengeance. There was even talk of tornadoes touching down in some areas. The hurricane ravaged the area, uprooting trees, flooding homes and businesses and leaving thousands without power.

"Wow." All Zoe could do was shake her head. She

and Ethan continued to wait for updates from the stations. For a long time, it didn't look like any trains were pulling out at all.

After she and Ethan had been waiting well over an hour and a departure time for her train still hadn't been posted, Zoe was beginning to believe she wasn't going to make it home. She called to check on her mother and sister. Fortunately they were safe in her mother's house.

"Keep us posted, honey. Let us know what's happening. Come here if it's easier for you than getting home."

"Thanks, Ma! I'll let you know."

Zoe ended her call and huffed. What if she couldn't get out of the city? She'd have to stay at a hotel. She didn't have any close friends in Manhattan.

She and Ethan listened to more news and continued checking the board for any updates on departures. Each time an announcement blared over the PA system, she prayed they would mention her train. Instead they announced more cancellations and delays.

"Any updates on your train?" she asked Ethan at last.

"No, but I'll be okay. I have an apartment here in the city if I can't get back home," he admitted. "I lived downtown while attending grad school and decided to keep the place after graduating. I go there sometimes after work or if I don't feel like heading to Long Island after hanging out late. You're welcome to stay there if you'd like. I don't keep the refrigerator or cabinets as well stocked as I do my home on Long Island but there's enough to get by."

"Thanks for the offer, but I'll figure something out." Zoe was grateful but didn't think staying at her good-looking boss's house was the best idea.

Her phone rang. It was Jasmine. "Hey. How's it going?"

"I can't hear you!" Jasmine said.

Zoe repeated herself more loudly. Penn Station was now filled to the brim with panicking riders worrying about getting home to kids and pets.

"I just got off the train." Jasmine was yelling into the phone. "The parking lot is flooded. I've never seen anything like this before. I'm wading through water to get to my car now. How are you making out?"

Zoe huffed. "I'm still at Penn Station. Only a few trains left right after yours. Nothing else has moved since then. It's been well over an hour."

"Oh my goodness. What are you going to do? If they don't start letting trains through soon, you'll have to get a room, Zoe!"

"Ugh. What a nightmare. I'm hoping this passes through as quickly as it came."

"You and me both," Jasmine said.

"Text me when you're home safe."

"Okay. And you let me know if you make it home or end up staying in the city," Jasmine insisted.

"Will do." Zoe shook her head before adding, "Have a good weekend despite the weather."

"I prepared, so let's hope all goes well."

"Okay. Talk to you later." Zoe ended the call. She had to figure out her next move. "Ethan, you don't have to wait on me. If these trains don't start moving soon, I'll get a hotel for the night." She smiled at him. "I appreciate you making sure I'm okay, but I don't want to hold you up any longer. You could be warm, safe and dry in your apartment by now. Oh! And how'd your brother and father make out?"

"Don't worry about me," he insisted. "I want to make sure you're okay. I just spoke to Brian. He made it to his mother's house. Carter and Dad are fine. Carter jumped on the subway to his place in downtown Brooklyn and Dad made it across the Williamsburg Bridge just before it was shut down due to winds and flooding."

"The Williamsburg was shut down?" Zoe asked in disbelief. This truly was another superstorm.

"Yep. Can't believe it. The news said some subway stations were closed due to flooding, as well."

"Whoa." She shook her head. It seemed that she'd definitely have to spend the night in Manhattan. She looked around at the crowded train station. All she could see were tightly packed people for yards.

"Listen. You go ahead and try to make it to your apartment before you get stuck," she said again. "I'm going to head to one of these nearby hotels and get a room. I need to move quick before all these people start filling up the vacancies."

"It's fine. I want to make sure you're okay," he repeated.

The sincerity in his tone was touching. Despite her telling him she'd be fine on her own, she was glad he was staying with her. Not being able to get home was unsettling. She tried hard to keep it together.

A woman next to her was frantically crying into her cell phone about having no one to pick up her daughter from day care. It made Zoe want to cry with her. Poor woman. Poor child. Being stuck was bad enough. She couldn't imagine being stuck and unable to get to her children. She wanted to help the woman but what could she possibly do? They were in the same position.

Though Zoe had never suffered from the condition, she now understood what claustrophobia felt like. The air felt thick. She had to get out of that station so she could breathe.

Ethan was still by her side.

"Let's get out of here," she told him at last. "I need to find a room."

"Okay." He immediately grabbed her hand and led the way through the dense crowd of people in Penn Station.

Outside, the rain came down in sheets. Zoe pulled her umbrella from her bag, but the moment she opened it, the wind took it away. She watched in disbelief as it tumbled down Thirty-Fourth Street. The forceful winds threatened to treat her the same way.

"Come on." Ethan tugged, leading her by the arm.

The stoplight turned green and they headed across the street to the Hotel Pennsylvania. Cars lined up along Seventh Avenue as far as they could see. Windshield wipers swung rapidly, sending water into the air. Despite the short distance between the station and the hotel, Zoe and Ethan were drenched when they reached the lobby.

Zoe couldn't believe her ears when the woman at the registration desk said they were already out of rooms. Between the conference they were hosting and the people who'd booked rooms because they couldn't get out of the city, the hotel had no vacancies left.

"Let's go over here." Ethan led her across the lobby to a corner that wasn't overcome with people trying to stay dry. "Let's call some of the other hotels in the area. We can also try checking in online."

"That's a good idea. I'll call some and if you don't mind, can you check others online?"

"Sure." Ethan began swiping away at his cell phone.

Zoe was so grateful for his presence. She pulled up local hotels and began making calls. Each one said they were at capacity.

"This travel app seems to have a few vacancies." Ethan turned his phone around so she could see the display.

Zoe pulled up the same app on her phone and booked a room a few blocks away. Ethan headed back outside to hail a taxi. It took at least twenty minutes for an empty one to pass by. The hotel was just a few blocks north on Eighth Avenue, but it took another half hour to make it there. Had it not been for the ball-size raindrops, they could have walked and gotten there faster.

They finally arrived at the hotel only to be told they didn't have any rooms available.

"But I have a confirmation!" Zoe waved her phone in the air. Her last bit of patience departed. "What do you mean you can't accept the reservation?"

The exhausted woman behind the counter explained that the app had somehow allowed the booking in error because there were absolutely no vacancies left. She explained how to request money back from the app.

Zoe couldn't believe this was happening to her. Then she thought about all those people down in Penn Station, still hoping to make it home.

"Look, Zoe," Ethan said at last. "This is not working out. Just come to my place. You'll be safe there. We'll grab something to eat and wait this out for a bit. Hopefully the trains will be back on track in a few more hours."

"Thank you, Ethan, but I'd hate to impose."

Imposing wasn't the problem. While it was fun to secretly crush on him, being with him in his Manhattan bachelor pad was just too much.

"It's not a problem. Let's go."

"I don't know…"

"Then what are you going to do?" he asked. "If we stay out here any longer, we'll both get sick."

Zoe huffed. What was she going to do? She had been

completely soaked from head to toe for a while now and had begun shivering. "Let me try a few more hotels."

"Sure," Ethan said. "Let's try a few more."

Zoe called hotels outside of the immediate area, hoping she would have a better chance booking a room. Some still didn't have vacancies and others just weren't able to promise her a room over the phone because of the volume of hopefuls filling their lobbies.

Reluctantly, Zoe turned to Ethan and threw her hands up. She felt defeated and wished she could blink and magically appear in her own living room. "I guess it's your place."

"Come on." He took her by the hand again and maneuvered out of the crowded hotel back into the heavy rain. "Let's hope we get a taxi faster this time."

The rain pelted them like darts. After a long while, they were finally able to get a taxi. The ride to SoHo took forever through flooded streets. Water ran down the windshield like someone was on top of the car pouring buckets over the glass.

Finally, they made it to Ethan's apartment building. Zoe was soaked down to her undergarments, her hair stuck to her face and her shoes squeaked when she walked across the lobby floor. But once she stepped inside his apartment, the beauty of it made her momentarily forget all she'd just waded through.

Ethan's place was stunning with an airy vibe. Dark wood floors made a striking contrast against stark white walls adorned with huge canvases of beautifully framed art. The stylish yet masculine decor brought together strong, dark colors against warm and creamy hues. Navy blue sofas held ivory pillows on one end and gray pillows on the other. The space opened to a kitchen with all of the cabinets and appliances aligning one wall and a massive granite-topped island setting the space apart from the living room. Next to the kitchen sat a dining table with places for six.

"Here. Let me take your coat," Ethan offered.

Zoe peeled it off and handed it to him. She felt a rush of coolness and hugged herself to ward off the chill. She looked up at the lofty exposed ceilings. Through the fully windowed wall, the storm looked like a beautiful but unsettling work of art. She took off her soggy shoes and walked around slowly.

"It's beautiful in here," she said finally.

"Thanks. I'll see if I can find you something dry to put on or at least get you some blankets. Then I'll see what I have in the freezer that I can defrost. There's probably not much more than water and butter in the fridge. I'm sure I have pasta and a few jars of sauce somewhere."

"Okay." Zoe heard him but never took her focus off of admiring the space.

Moments later, he emerged with a hoodie and sweats that were sure to be too large for her.

"You can change in that bedroom or the bathroom down there on the right." Ethan pointed.

Zoe released a heavy sigh. "Thanks, Ethan." She went into the bathroom, which was clad in marble from the ceiling to the floor. A floating vanity with a stone sink boasted contemporary faucets, making the small bathroom look like something straight out of a fancy hotel. She peeled off her wet clothes, leaving just her underwear, and put on the oversize sweats Ethan had given her. They were big, soft and dry and for that she was grateful.

She put her belongings in the spare room he'd offered, then headed back to the living area and found Ethan already changed.

She was used to him looking handsome in tailored suits, but Zoe wasn't ready for how rugged and sexy Ethan would be in simple sweats and a college T-shirt. His taut chest strained against the university's logo. The short sleeves exposed muscular arms wrapped in smooth brown skin. She watched his muscles shift and flex as he pulled food from the freezer. Not knowing what to do with herself, Zoe joined him in the kitchen.

"Can I help?" she asked pensively, not wanting to get too close. The pressure of being alone with him at his place was both stimulating and nerve-racking. Still, she'd had no choice, she reasoned.

"You like burgers and fries?" he asked. "I found some ground turkey in the freezer."

"Turkey works for me"

"Cool. No help needed. Why don't you find something on TV? I'll whip up one of my gourmet burgers for you. I found some good bread in the fridge."

Again she thought about how grateful she was that Ethan had waited with her. What would she have done if he'd gone home and left her alone at Penn Station? She might have ended up sleeping on a bench.

Zoe called her mother and sister to let them know she was safe and had gone to a "friend's" house in the city to ride out the storm. They were glad to hear that she was okay.

She pointed the remote at the television and found a news station to get more updates on the weather. Hopefully she'd be able to head home in a few hours.

She glanced back at Ethan in the kitchen. He was humming as he patted out the burgers. She'd never been in an apartment like this before or with a man like him, and for just a moment, she allowed her imagination to roam. What would it be like to actually be the girlfriend of Ethan Blackwell?

Ten

"What did you do to that burger?" Zoe asked, popping the last fry in her mouth. "That was amazing."

"Can't tell you." Ethan kept his eyes on the television with his feet comfortably propped on an ottoman.

Zoe gave him a sideways glance. Ethan laughed. She looked beautiful even when she shot him sketchy looks.

"I have to give you credit," she said. "It was great. I didn't peg you for a cook."

"You figured I was spoiled." He let the assumption hang in the air.

Zoe remained quiet. After several moments ticked away in silence, she offered up a puppy dog look. "Guilty as charged," she finally admitted.

"You do karate and change tires. I cook—among other things—*and* change tires."

Zoe shrugged. "I misjudged you."

"Yep. You did. Consider us even, though. I misjudged you, too. I was surprised you knew so much about cars."

"Surprise!" Zoe chuckled. It was like a soft melody.

He smiled. Not because of the funny way she'd said *surprise*, but because the sound of her laughter gave him a sense of joy.

Her perfectly plump lips made Ethan want to reach over and kiss her. Instead, he got up, took her empty plate, placed it on top of his and headed to the kitchen. "Want a refill on your iced tea?"

"Sure."

Ethan stayed in the kitchen longer than necessary. He had to put some distance between Zoe and himself. Being close to her was wreaking havoc on his will. Having her all to himself like this when she was completely off-limits was taking a toll on him.

He studied her for a quick moment as she took in the news. Her hair had dried some. Even his oversize clothing looked good on her. Her frizzy tresses and the sight of his clothes on her shapely body made his imagination run wild. Zoe looked a sexy mess.

After a while, he returned with the jug of iced tea and poured more in her cup, set the jug down and turned up the volume on the television. Updates on the train system would be a safe distraction.

"I need to—" Zoe turned to him to speak but stopped abruptly when she noticed him studying her. She cleared her throat "—let my mom know I'll be home later than I thought."

He smiled. "Sure." Then sat back and returned his focus to the news.

Zoe stood, grabbed her cell phone and called her mother. She paced the kitchen as she talked. From what Ethan overheard, her family seemed to be fine.

While she spoke to them, he reached for his phone and dialed 311, New York City's service line. He asked about transportation updates in an attempt to get more information for Zoe. To his surprise, Manhattan was completely cut off from the other boroughs. The bridges were shut down because of strong winds, and tunnels, stations and streets were flooded all over the metropolitan area. Sporadic power and out-of-order streetlights caused traffic debacles. Trees were down everywhere.

Ethan ended his call and turned up the volume on the TV. The mayor was declaring a state of emergency, and authorities encouraged everyone to stay inside until the storm passed. Soggy newscasters, out on location and covered by ineffective raincoats, reported on the extreme weather conditions as they were pelted by large raindrops and jostled by the wind. Their cameras showed scenes of people taking shelter inside restaurants and stores. Stranded commuters were packed in bus and train stations across the city.

Ethan looked out his lofty windows. A brooding darkness loomed across the sky. As if on cue, lightning flashed and thunder rolled, making Zoe flinch where she stood in the kitchen. Ethan wished he could hold her in his arms.

This storm didn't look like it was passing anytime soon. Even if it did, how soon would transportation get back up and running? Maybe the bridges would open first. He could drive Zoe home with the car he kept in the garage below the apartment building. But what about those flooded streets?

Zoe ended her call and came back to sit on the couch.

"I have good news and not so good news," Ethan began.

"Okay." She stretched the word with curiosity.

"Which do you want first?"

"Hit me with the bad news," she said, throwing up

her hands. "It can't get much worse than it already is, can it?"

"Well…" Ethan sighed. "I don't think you're going to get home tonight."

She groaned. He shared the information he'd gathered from 311 and the news.

"This is horrible," she grumbled. "I never thought I'd see anything like this in New York again."

"I know. Me, too." A few moments of silence passed as they absorbed this reality.

"So what's the good news?" Zoe finally asked.

"You're welcome to say here for the night."

Zoe stiffened at once.

"If you're okay with it," he rushed. "I'm concerned that you won't get a room anywhere at this point." He sensed how uncomfortable this made her. As her boss, he understood. "You can sleep in the spare room. If the trains still aren't running in the morning, I can drive you home. I keep one of my cars here for when I stay over."

"You…" Zoe cleared her throat. "Are you sure you don't mind?"

"Do you have a better option?"

Zoe looked around as if she'd find a better option right there in the room. "I guess not."

"Besides food, we have Netflix, a deck of cards and a DVD player."

"Wait! A what? Who still has a DVD player?" Zoe's eyes widened and she chuckled.

"I do!" Ethan said confidently. "It's Blu-ray with Wi-Fi, Netflix, Amazon Prime and YouTube. Sometimes I want to watch movies that aren't on Netflix or Prime. I have a few old favorites that I can watch whenever I want to."

"Okay." She nodded approvingly. "Now that I think

of it, that's not such a bad idea. I can't stand it when I want to watch something and can't find it on any of those services. You're a smart guy after all, Ethan."

"I am pretty smart." He stood, puffed his chest and strutted over to his bookshelf.

"You're hilarious, too."

He laughed, relaxed his posture and picked up a few DVDs, shuffling through them. "Come see if there's anything you want to watch."

Zoe hopped up from the couch and joined him as he sifted through his movie collection. She seemed more comfortable now. A bit cheery, even. He was glad. He didn't want her to feel uncomfortable. She might be off-limits, but he'd never deny enjoying her company. The fact that he was going to be able to continue enjoying her presence tonight made him smile. But misbehaving wasn't an option, no matter how kissable her lips looked.

"You have so many older movies," she commented.

Ethan reached for the movie she held, the first in the *Fast & Furious* franchise. "There's a new *Fast & Furious* movie coming this year. I can watch the entire series and get ready for the latest installment."

"I love that franchise," she confessed. "That's actually what I did before the latest *Avengers* movie came out. And you're right, I had to get creative in order to find some of the earlier movies." She paused a moment, tilting her head. "I think it might be time to buy myself a DVD player."

"See what I mean?" Ethan nodded.

They fell silent for a bit while Zoe went through the movie collection.

"So, did you decide on anything you'd like to watch?" he asked after she'd put a few aside.

"A few things. Let me narrow down my choices. Oh!"

Her sudden excitement caught Ethan's attention. "*Avatar*! I loved that movie. Wanna watch that?"

He shrugged. "Let's do it."

Zoe handed him the movie, and he inserted it into the player, then made his way back to the couch with the remote.

"Something to drink before the movie starts?" he asked. "Truthfully, I don't have much more than some soda and several choice bottles of wine." Ethan thought for a moment. "Not sure if you're a scotch drinker. I do have some choice scotch and a nice bourbon."

Zoe chuckled. "I had a former boss who drank scotch. She said her father taught her to appreciate it and that resulted in her being respected by some of the most prominent businessmen in the world."

"It sounds crazy but it's true. A woman who knows and can handle a good scotch is one to be reckoned with."

Zoe chuckled. "You don't seem to have much in the way of regular food here, do you?"

"Guilty." He held his hands up. "I'm usually here to entertain so I never run out of spirits. Scotch or wine?"

"I'll start with wine," Zoe said.

"Okay. Red or white?"

"Red."

"Oh. Bold. I like it."

"Yes. It's even better with chocolate—especially dark chocolate."

"I definitely don't have any chocolate here."

"Didn't think so. Would have been nice."

Yes, Ethan thought as he selected a nice cab and poured her a glass. It would have been really nice to feed her chocolate between sips. But that wasn't what

Zoe was there for. She wasn't his company to entertain in that way.

He wondered what it would be like to date a girl like her. She was nothing like any woman he'd ever been with. Of course they, too, had been smart, confident, ambitious, fashionable and so much more—just not in the way that Zoe was. She owned and exuded each adjective in ways he'd never seen before. Most women he knew wouldn't touch a tire, let alone change it. Zoe's confidence didn't border on conceit. She was sure and comfortable with who she was. Plain and simple. She was also sexy in a natural way. She didn't put sexy on like a cloak and try to convince the world of her appeal. She just was. Her appeal was effortless. That was what intrigued him most.

Ethan wondered why she didn't seem to have a boyfriend. He hadn't asked. Of course it would have been inappropriate since he was her boss, but he wanted to know. There was so much he wanted to know about Zoe, but he had to tread carefully.

"… Ethan?"

"Yes." He realized she'd called his name more than once. He poured himself a glass of wine and pushed away those thoughts.

"You're with me?"

"Yeah. Just thinking…that's all." He stopped there, unable to share more. "Ready." He held up the remote, his thumb hovering over the play button.

"Ready! I love this movie. Haven't seen it in so long."

"Here goes." He pushed the button. For the next two hours and forty-plus minutes, they remained enthralled in the decade-old blockbuster movie, polished off two more glasses of wine and munched on chips and a few other snacks that Ethan found hiding in his pantry.

The movie ended, leaving them in a limbo of awkward quiet. He looked at his watch. It was just past nine.

"Let's see what the news is saying about the storm now."

Ethan flipped to the news. They took in several moments of reporting from various stations, all of them saying the same thing. This storm was categorized as the most severe storm of the decade, and despite how much the city had prepared, New York just hadn't been ready for the resulting damage. And the storm wasn't over. The mayor detailed all that the city was doing to help residents navigate through this disaster. Most important for Ethan and Zoe, trains still weren't running and the bridges had yet to open. Zoe definitely wasn't getting home tonight.

Ethan muted the TV, quieting the bad news. He and Zoe sat back on the couch at the same time, looked at each other and acknowledged their twin behavior with a smile.

"Another movie?" he asked.

"Where are those cards you had? Ever play War?"

"War?" He scrunched his nose curiously.

"Yes. Get the cards. It's a little silly, but fun."

Ethan was much more of a poker player but was happy to indulge her. He got up from the couch and headed over to the same shelf that held his DVDs. When he returned, he handed her the cards. Zoe shuffled them.

"Okay. My sister and I used to play all the time when we were kids. We start with the same number of cards, keep them facedown and turn them over only when it's time to play a card. Whoever plays the highest card gets to take two cards that were already played and add them to their deck. If we play the same card, then we declare war, playing one card per word, 'I. Declare. War.'" She demonstrated, laying down three cards as she spoke. "Whoever plays the highest card on the word *war* takes all the cards played. You win by getting all the cards. Got it?"

"I think so." Ethan furrowed his brows.

"It's easier than it sounds. Come on." Zoe dealt the cards and taught him as they played.

Once he got the hang of it, he played more aggressively, raising the stakes. The intensity made both of them more competitive. They opened two more bottles of wine, adding to what they'd shared during the movie, loosening their tongues, evoking a more comfortable, uninhibited vibe between them.

"Ha! Got you that time." Ethan thrust both hands in the air after winning and boasted, "War."

"Beginner's luck."

"No luck. That's skill!"

"Really, Ethan? That would make sense if you could actually see what card you're playing. The cards are facedown when you pull them, silly."

She laughed at him, and he couldn't help but join in.

They played several more games, talking trash and mocking one another when they won, slamming down winning cards, grunting and groaning their losses, having unadulterated, tipsy fun.

Next, Zoe taught Ethan how to play a game called Spit—another two-player game that required quick thinking, coordination and speed. The wine they drank hindered all three, causing them to exude more laughter than skill.

A few games in, Zoe was in the lead. Ethan had repositioned himself to better grab the smaller stack of cards, but he still moved too slow and Zoe grabbed the stack. The larger pile was now Ethan's hand, bringing him closer to losing the game. Now they were down to their last play of the latest game.

Ethan sat leaning forward, ready to slam his hand down and claim his victory. He played several cards. Zoe slipped in and played a few from her hand. He watched intently, keeping an eye on how many cards she had left. She was down to two. If Zoe hit the empty spot first, she'd score another win. If Ethan beat her to it, he was back in the game and would have another chance. He readied his hand to hit the empty pile.

Zoe played her very last card.

Time seemed to move in slow motion.

She raised her hand. Ethan raised his. Both aimed for the empty spot, in a race to secure the win or get back in the game. Zoe's hand reach the floor a split second before Ethan's, and his hand landed on top of hers.

For a brief electrifying moment, all his senses converged. All he could feel was a pulsing sensation that shot through his hand on top of hers. In that millisecond, he felt how soft her skin was and wished he could continue touching her.

The moment was over as quickly as it began.

Zoe rapidly slid her hand from under his, jumped to her feet and thrust both arms triumphantly in the air. "I win again!" She rolled her arms in front of her in a Cabbage Patch dance, singing "I'm a winner" over and over again. She switched up her dance with some flossing and ended with a dab.

After her silly display, she plopped back down on the couch, and all Ethan could do was laugh. He wasn't used to losing but the sweet sound of her joy made him want to see her win every moment of every day. Her laugh seemed to erupt from the center of her core, and he loved the sound of it. Enjoying her glee, he watched her. Watched her plump lips part, framing a perfect set of teeth. Watched the sensual line of her neck as she threw her head back. Watched her tresses bounce as her shoulders shook. Watched her eyes sparkle with joy. He noticed her smooth, glowing skin.

His hand moved without instructions from his brain. He responded to a need that compelled him, and he gently touched her cheek with the backs of his fingers.

Zoe's laughter subsided. Her eyes locked with Ethan's. No words passed between them. None were needed; all the desire they'd tried to contain seemed to take over, pulling them to one another. Instinct took over. Inch by inch, they drew closer, mouths parted, ready for each other.

Ethan's eyes closed seconds before their lips connected, and electricity exploded inside of him. He wrapped his arms around her, and she placed her hands on his face, pulled him in and kissed him harder.

They kissed like they had been starved and their lips were the only thing that could satisfy their hunger. He didn't want to let her go. She clung to him as if she felt the same. They kissed until they had to stop just so they could breathe.

Eleven

Zoe opened her eyes in time to glimpse the warm hues of the sunrise through floor-to-ceiling windows. She looked around and tried to blink the confusion away. Obviously, she wasn't at home. Where was she? It took a few moments to gather her wits about her. She looked around once more and remembered.

The memories appeared before her in flashes—breaking news, thunder, lightning, the *Avatar* movie, playing cards, wine and the kiss. Instinctively, she touched her lips, remembering how his lips on hers had taken her breath away. She had kissed her boss. Zoe closed her eyes. She shook her head. She'd kissed her boss and loved it! If she were honest with herself, she'd admit she wanted to do it all over again.

At that memory, Zoe closed her eyes and let her head fall back. She felt sluggish with a slight headache.

Lifting her head, she scanned the posh, spacious living area. She never had made it to that second bedroom. Nor had Ethan made it to his. He was sprawled out on the floor near the couch where Zoe slept. How much did they drink?

A hint of panic settled in. She had always been careful not to drink too much when she was with coworkers. That had proved to be a dangerous choice for colleagues in the past. She never wanted to have to take that walk of shame through the office after doing too much at a company event.

The spectacular colors of the sunrise caught her eye once more. Instead of panicking, Zoe decided to take the moment to enjoy watching the sun come up. With the position of Ethan's apartment and the height of his floor, the view was unhindered. She took a deep breath and simply watched. Zoe was a born-and-bred New Yorker, yet she'd never seen a sunrise from this perspective.

The urge to relieve herself hit her fiercely. As quietly as possible, she slid off the couch, picked up her phone and tiptoed to the bathroom without waking Ethan. She thought about last night. She'd actually had a great time with him. The initial discomfort she'd felt about sharing such intimate space with her boss had passed as the night went on—with help from the wine, of course. She'd been warm, dry and safe. What more could she ask for?

Zoe wondered about all those people who had been stranded at the train and bus stations. What had happened to them? What about the parents who couldn't get to their children? She said a quick silent prayer for those impacted by the storm.

She stayed in the bathroom to check in on her mother and sister. She didn't want to wake Ethan with her conversation. "Hey, Ma. How are things going?"

"Not too bad, considering." Laura sighed. "Our lights went out last night."

"Ugh! Did they say when they will be back on?"

"No. How about you? Still in the city?"

"Yeah. Couldn't get out yesterday. No one was supposed to be on the roads. I'm hoping I can get home today."

"This is truly something, isn't it? I'm glad we went shopping before all this started."

"I'm glad, too. You have food. I would have been going nuts over here if you didn't."

"Thank God. When you get out of the city, don't worry about coming here," Laura insisted. "We're going to be fine. Go home and check your place. See if you have electricity. I've been listening to the radio all morning. The damage is bad. Power lines are down. Trees have fallen on cars and houses. And some of the train stations...whew! The news showed video of water flowing down the steps like someone was pouring out a jug. The commuter rails have flooding up to the platforms. You could actually see fish swimming in the tracks!"

"Wow!"

"I know."

For several moments, Zoe and her mother were simply silent, the only sound the two of them breathing. Zoe was glad that the worst of the damages her mother had experienced was a power outage.

"Okay, Ma. I'll let you know when I leave here."

"Keep me posted."

"Will do."

Zoe ended the call with her mother and dialed a neighbor. She wasn't particularly close with any of her neighbors, but they did look out for each other. Her neighbor said that, like Laura's area, their town house complex had lost power, and listed all the other damage the storm had done in their community. Zoe thought about all the food she'd have to toss because of the loss of electricity. She shook her head and decided to save that worry for when she got home.

She noticed that Ethan had left a folded towel, face cloth, toothbrush and travel-size bottle of mouthwash on a small shelf inside the bathroom. She freshened up, then walked back out to the living area to be greeted by the mouthwatering aroma of fine coffee. She could also smell a hint of vanilla. She didn't see Ethan, but she heard the faint sounds of a shower running behind his closed bedroom door.

Zoe headed to the kitchen and poured steaming coffee into a mug that Ethan had obviously set out for her. She topped it off with creamer and returned to the living room to get the latest updates on the news.

The storm had passed, but the city was still paralyzed due to the damage it had left in its wake. Bridges and tunnels were still closed. Businesses and residences alike were running on backup generators due to all the power lines that were down. Transformers had actually caught fire in the rain. It was going to take a while for the city to recover.

Zoe had no idea when she'd be able to make it home, but she tried to remain hopeful. She'd already survived one night in her boss's private domain.

Still, she hoped she didn't have to stay at Ethan's place another night. Besides not wanting to be an imposition, being this close to him challenged her ability to focus. She was used to seeing him in business attire. Seeing his taut body in a T-shirt and sweats with bare feet showed him in a whole different light, one that was laid-back, comfortable and incredibly sexy. Zoe had only hoped he hadn't caught her taking in his pecs and biceps. By contrast, she had on his clothes and was sure she looked a frumpy mess.

She had seen many sides of Ethan yesterday. She loved how he'd taken charge and insisted that she let him help her, all to ensure she'd be okay. Zoe had always loved a man keen enough to wield the right balance of humor, wit and consideration. They'd had fun last night. His playful and competitive demeanor teased her. His concern for her safety warmed her. His thoughtfulness moved her.

All of these things were reasons for her to get out of his place as soon as possible.

Zoe curled up on the couch, sipped from her coffee cup and refocused her attention on the news.

"Good morning."

Ethan's rich voice startled her. It sounded a bit lower than usual, causing a slight squiggle to curl down her back. She chalked it up to him being tired just like she was. She swallowed quickly. "Oh! Hey. Good morning." She tried to appear unaffected.

"I didn't mean to startle you. How's the coffee?"

She took another sip. "Delicious."

"Good."

Ethan walked into the kitchen, opened the refrigerator and pulled out eggs and a few other items. "I hope you like frittatas."

"I do."

"Good. There's not much more in here for breakfast. We can do that and some toast with water and coffee?"

"Sounds great to me."

Zoe watched as he worked his way around the large island, pulling out pans and preparing to cook. He had on a different T-shirt and sweats than the night before but looked just as sexy. His body boasted of a regular workout regimen. And even from the couch, he smelled fresh and amazing. She took in a long sniff. His oaky scent mixed with her French vanilla coffee was delightful.

"Can I help?" The words came out before she realized she'd offered. "You've already done so much. The least I could do is help with breakfast."

"Sure."

Zoe unfolded her legs, got up off the couch and joined him in the kitchen. In silence, they worked seamlessly together as if they'd cooked this way every day. She finished whipping the eggs while Ethan chopped veggies before tossing them into the hot frying pan. They had a rhythm and it worked well.

The only disruptions were the moments where they accidentally touched, causing tingling sensations to crawl over Zoe's skin. She hoped she was the only one to feel those tingles. She remembered their kiss and shivered, hoping he hadn't noticed.

It helped that he was off-limits. Zoe didn't mind crushing on Ethan; it made working with him fun. But she had never in a million years thought of acting on any of it. She loved and needed her job.

"It's still pretty bad out there but I'll be out of your hair today," she said, breaking the silence. "Thanks so much for putting me up last night."

"I saw the reports while I was getting dressed," Ethan said. "You still might not be able to get home today."

She sighed. "Yeah. But don't you worry. I'll be out of your hair either way."

"Zoe." The way Ethan called her name caused her breath to catch. His voice held so much concern. He turned to look at her and she almost couldn't stand the caring but penetrating way he looked at her. "It's dangerous out there. You're welcome to stay another night. Really, it's not a problem. And I have the room."

"Uh…um…" She cleared her throat. "You've done enough, Ethan. I appreciate it so much, but I need to try to get home and deal with what the storm left for me there."

He looked pensive for a quick moment. "Okay. I'll do what I can to help. If we can get across any of the bridges or through the tunnels, I'll drive you home. We can assess our options after we eat."

The two returned to silence and finished preparing the few items they had for breakfast. The frittatas were tasty and all they had to wash down the food was water and coffee. When they were done, Ethan made some calls to see about being able to get back to Long Island. He took a few of those calls in his room behind closed doors. Zoe wondered if he was speaking to a lady friend.

Unfortunately, a way home did not reveal itself. The roadways were still shut down, the trains weren't running yet and authorities were still assessing the damage. Cars were stuck in water along some of the major highways and downed lines made traveling through water dangerous. A number of people across the area had suffered electric shocks.

"What now?" Zoe asked once they'd cleaned up after breakfast.

"Movie?" Ethan took his coffee and plopped on the couch. He pointed the remote at the television.

"Or I could beat you in another game of cards."

"Ha!" Ethan threw his head back. "This time, I'll teach you a few games."

"Bring it on."

He grabbed the deck of cards and showed her a new

game that he and his siblings used to play, a game where players had to constantly call each other's bluffs.

"All right," he began. "It's called BS."

Zoe raised a brow and tilted her head to the side. "BS. As in bull—"

"Yep," Ethan interjected. "When you suspect your opponent of bluffing, you have to call out BS."

"Did your parents know you were playing this?"

"My grandmother taught it to us!"

Zoe laughed hard. "I like your grandma."

They played the game for the next hour or so and by the time they stopped for lunch, Zoe's belly hurt from laughing so much. Once she got the hang of the game, she bluffed a lot and Ethan called her out on her bluffing just as much.

At one point, he turned up the television and they got updates on the aftermath of the weather before picking another movie to watch.

He called a few local restaurants to see if any were open for them to order dinner. Fortunately a few were, and they ordered his favorite Asian takeout.

After spending the past twenty-four hours together in close quarters, the atmosphere between them had settled into a more comfortable existence. Zoe felt it in her posture. Ethan's feet rested on the ottoman in front of him. She folded her feet under her as she picked fresh popcorn from a bowl. They flowed between laughter and conversation with ease. Subjects that they'd been careful not to broach before became a familiar part of their dialogue. Zoe felt like she and Ethan had been old friends for years—almost.

He looked at her and cocked his head sideways.

Her hand paused midway as she was bringing a piece of popcorn to her mouth. "What?" she asked.

"So, why don't you have a boyfriend?"

Zoe shrugged. "I can't blame it all on men. I haven't always made a good girlfriend."

Ethan reared his head back. "What makes you say that?"

"It's what I've been told," she said, matter-of-fact. "More than once."

His eyes widened. "Wow."

She waved dismissively. "That doesn't bother me." She laughed. "Well, not anymore." She handed him the popcorn. He took the bowl and dug in. "I've been accused of acting—" she made air quotes "—like a man." She sniffed. "One said I was too ambitious because I paid more attention to my career and not enough to him. I guess that summed up what most of them felt and honestly, I just didn't know what to do with that. My career means a lot to me. I spend a lot of time focusing on it and then there's my family."

Zoe stopped talking. She wasn't ready to talk intimately about her family with Ethan. He didn't need to know about her family's battle with Shena's mental illness.

"Seems like selfishness on their part."

"Eh. Sometimes it was hard for me to balance both. I worked really hard on my past jobs to earn my bosses' respect and set myself up for potential promotions. Whenever I didn't get a promotion, it made me work harder to prove myself for the next time. In the process, my relationships suffered. I didn't mean for it to happen that way."

"You didn't have the right men."

Zoe looked at him curiously.

"They should have been supporting you and celebrating your determination instead of getting upset about you working hard to get somewhere."

That was how she felt, too, but she remained quiet. Ethan was the first man who had ever said anything like that to her. The others just complained about how little they got from her.

"In my opinion," he went on, "it's obvious that they were threatened by your potential."

"I guess." She tilted her head, thankful for his apparent appreciation of her ambition.

"I bet you weren't as bad a girlfriend as you thought."

His deep gaze made something shift inside of her. She swallowed and smiled. "Thanks, Ethan. I'll remember that."

"Their loss. Lucky me," he said, taking the empty bowl to the island. He came to sit near her on the couch.

"How are you lucky?"

"Your boss's failure to give you the chance you deserve is what led you to our company. You're definitely an asset—hardworking, brilliant, savvy, full of great ideas and you deliver. It's why I hired you. Someone would have to be blind not to see what you bring to the table."

A smile slowly spread across her face. Zoe felt her cheeks warm. It was almost as if he'd said he loved her. Her previous boss had never complimented her or praised her work. Not once. "Thank you, Ethan."

"I mean that."

The lights flickered and she yelped. "What was that?"

Ethan huffed and jumped up from the couch. "I hope it's not what I think it is."

The lights flickered again. She folded her knees to her chest, praying that the power wouldn't go completely out.

Suddenly they heard a thud and everything went black.

Twelve

The only light in the apartment came from the dim evening sky. Soon, all they would have was the moonlight.

Ethan called Maintenance, who explained that flooding in the basement was causing sporadic outages in the building and the backup generator couldn't keep up. The only active lighting was the emergency lighting in the hallways.

Ethan had bought a loft in this particular building because of the older charm and larger room sizes, but it also meant it didn't have some of the latest technologies like newer structures did. The technician assured Ethan that help was on the way and that they would be working diligently to restore power to the building. This also meant they couldn't use the elevator, so they were stuck inside the building unless they wanted to walk up and down several flights of stairs. Until then, he and Zoe would have to remain in the dark.

Ethan groaned as he ended the call. He looked at his phone. Since he'd spent most of his time watching movies, playing cards and talking with Zoe, he still had pretty good battery life. He relayed the info from Maintenance to Zoe.

"Wow! What else could go wrong?"

"Hey, shh! Don't say that."

"You're right. Or the universe will show me what else could go wrong. My bad." She laughed.

"How's the battery in your phone?" he asked.

"Pretty good. Yours?"

"About eighty percent."

"I have my portable charger in my handbag, too. Do you have one here?"

"I don't." He huffed.

"What about candles? Do you have any around?"

Ethan pressed his lips together and thought for a moment. "I might." He'd used this place for entertaining plenty of women; he was bound to have a few candles inside a drawer somewhere. He checked the kitchen and linen closets and came back with a few. He lined them up on the kitchen island and pulled out a lighter.

"No!" Zoe held her hands up. "We still have a bit of sunlight. Let's wait until we really need them."

Ethan was grateful to still have her company. "See. Smart lady."

"Oh, Ethan," she said in an exaggerated tone. "Flattery will get you everywhere." They laughed, easing the intensity of the moment.

Ethan sat back down on the couch. The shadows and light from the descending sun cast her face in a mysterious glow. She looked even more beautiful.

"Where do you see yourself going after Blackwell?" he asked.

"Hmm." Zoe put her hand on her chin. "I'm hoping to be here for a while and learn as much as I can from you and your family. I'd love to make it to the C-suite one day."

They talked until the only light in the apartment came from a sliver of moonlight through the window and a few sporadically placed candles. Circumstances had created a romantic atmosphere that Ethan hadn't anticipated.

He fought to keep his focus on their conversation, but his attention kept drifting to her perfect silhouette. A time or two, perhaps three, they brushed against one another, unable to properly gauge their distance in the dim light. Each time, Ethan felt currents strong enough to light the room with his own fire surge along the places that she touched.

They talked and talked, familiarizing themselves with one another's life, getting comfortable in each other's presence. He asked question after question, eager to know things about Zoe that he hadn't known before. In spite of the inconvenience of the weather, he was secretly thankful for the time he was spending with her. It couldn't amount to much, but he enjoyed it nonetheless.

"What about you, Ethan? Why don't you have a girlfriend?" Zoe asked, tilting her head.

She'd brought the conversation back to that. "I did." Ethan sighed. "Like you, I've been accused of putting too much of my time and energy into work. We started working on the company's expansion a while back, way before we actually put any of our plans into action. I was working long days, spending weekends with my dad and the rest of the team strategizing and mapping things out. One afternoon, I decided I wanted to surprise my girlfriend and take her out, spend some time with her. I pulled up to her place and there was a man standing on her front steps. She opened the door, he swept her into his arms, kissed her and carried her inside. He used his foot to close the door."

"Oh! Ethan. I'm so sorry. What did you do?"

"I sat in the car fuming for a few moments before I realized that what we had was over long before that day. I got out of my car and used my key to get into her house. I followed their sounds toward her bedroom. The door was wide open. She obviously wasn't expecting me. I calmly walked in and said hello. She screamed. The two of them jumped out of the bed, covering their naked bodies with the sheets. It was obvious they hadn't wasted any time. Clothes were tossed across the floor from the door to the bed. I held up her key, placed it on the table next to her bed and walked out."

Zoe's eyes stretched wide. Her hand covered her mouth. "What did they do?"

"Nothing. They just watched me with their mouths wide open. I closed the front door, got in my car and went back to work."

"Oh my goodness, Ethan. That's terrible."

"Like I said, it was over way before it was officially over. The end was inevitable, so I wasn't totally surprised to see she had moved on to someone else. By the way, they're married now. Ha!"

"Whoa!"

Darkness had fully arrived, swallowing up the tense silence they fell into. Zoe reached over and touched Ethan's arm. "I'm so sorry about that. You're a catch. There's a woman out there that will appreciate the hardworking man that you are."

Ethan felt the electricity from her touch. He looked at her. "Of course," he said confidently. A smile eased across his lips and he took in her beauty; the candle's flickering light shimmered in her eyes. She looked radiant under the moonlight.

He imagined that the woman Zoe spoke of would be a lot like her. Despite all common sense, for a moment, he wished it could be her.

Her lips were perfect. Inviting. Ethan recalled the softness from their kiss. He wanted to kiss her again. The curve from her chin to her neck was the sexiest angle he'd ever set his eyes on. He recalled her confidence, and silly things like the fact that she could change tires. He didn't know many women like Zoe. The fact that it seemed like she didn't need a man at all intrigued him all the more.

She swallowed, and Ethan watched her neck shift in the soft light. Every maneuver came across as sensual. Her hand was still on his arm. He covered it with his hand. Electric sparks radiated in his palm.

Ethan took that hand and before he knew what he was doing, he kissed it. He found himself leaning toward her, and she drew closer to him. He felt controlled by an outside force, unable to resist the pull. She seemed compelled by the same force. His breath came in a rush.

They closed the space between them and paused once they were close enough to almost touch. They were still for a brief moment. Ethan contemplated the feel of her lips. He shouldn't. He wanted to. So badly. He fought the good fight against his will and lost.

Zoe reached out with her free hand and touched his face, pulling him closer. Closing the gap. Her caress ignited a fire that reasonable thoughts and common sense could not quench. Their lips connected.

Hers were so soft. Sweet but also salty from the popcorn. Perfect. Fireworks exploded in his head, danced and then consumed them both. The kiss was hot, deep, passionate and breathtaking. She moved closer and held his face with both her hands. Ethan wrapped his arms around her, pressing their bodies together.

The fire licked at them, sparking a hunger that refused to be doused. Their hands roamed every part of the other's body. All the restraint Ethan had exercised in her presence since the day he'd set eyes on her crumbled like a house made of cards. Desire scorched a hot path through him, and he felt his temperature rise. If he could trust his sense of touch, her body was blazing as much as his.

He couldn't get enough. He pulled his mouth from Zoe's long enough to take a breath, lacing her face with loving pecks before taking her lips fully again. They shifted positions, never truly disconnecting from each other, her body stretching out under his, her hands furiously exploring any area she could reach.

Ethan was careful not to apply too much pressure as he held himself over her. He could feel his erection strain against his sweats, pressing against her. Aware of how his desire surged over him, he reluctantly ended the kiss.

Several beats ticked by as the hastened rhythm of their thumping hearts slowed. Their chests rose and fell in the same declining tempo.

Ethan stared into her eyes. He could see the rawness of her longing. Zoe licked her kiss-swollen lips and he wanted to feel them again but resisted. He pushed himself up and sat back on the couch and tried to catch his breath. He fought to remove himself from her the way magnets fought to connect.

Zoe sat up beside him. She took his hand in hers,

breathing just as hard. Neither of them spoke. Together they sat there in the dark.

What had he just done?

Thirteen

Forget butterflies, something deeper fluttered in Zoe's stomach. Ethan—no, her *boss* had just kissed the breath out of her and all she could think about was kissing him again and again. She could see the inquiries behind his eyes. She knew that, like her, he was pondering what they'd just done.

She had just kissed her boss—again! She should have felt worse about it but didn't. It felt too good. Zoe felt like she was floating when his lips touched hers. She couldn't stop thinking about it after. Her mind had told her not to do it, but with one touch of his hand, she couldn't resist. She wanted more. Much more.

She put her hand back on his face, knowing he would understand the gesture as an invitation. He looked into her eyes and nodded. The air in her lungs swirled. She was breathless at the mere thought of tasting his lips once again. Hunger rose in her, and their lips met again.

The same urgency flared again, an all-consuming, desperate fire.

Caresses turned into tugs and pulls. Longing blazed a hot trail from her center up to her chest. Ethan pulled back from their intense kiss and stared into her eyes again as if seeking more permission. She gave it to him by rising up to kiss him.

"You're so beautiful," he said, breaking the kiss again to catch some air. "Tell me if you want me to stop." He spoke without taking his lips off of hers.

She kissed him back, meeting his increased tension with her own.

"Should I stop?" he asked, his voice a breathless whisper. "Tell me to stop." He kissed her deeply, and she moaned. "I will if you want me to. Tell me what you want," he said hoarsely, and Zoe felt the rumble of his voice in her belly.

"You," she said without fully breaking their kiss. He gave her an intense look, and she nodded. "I want you, Ethan. If you'll have me."

"I want you, Zoe, as long as it's all right with you."

"Yes." Her voice was soft and filled with desire even to her own ears.

Zoe didn't want to think about him being her boss. She didn't want to think about what tomorrow would bring. She no longer cared about not being at home. All that mattered in that moment was being with Ethan. Their attraction for one another was obvious and had been for quite a while. Since they'd arrived at his place the evening before, the chemistry between them had turned into smoke rising, becoming more dense as the hours passed. Now it practically suffocated them. It couldn't be ignored. Denying it hadn't worked.

Zoe had dreamed of this. They were two experienced,

grown, consenting adults. She decided not to expect much after this night. It would be their one night together.

"Just this one night," she said, convinced that was all she needed to quench the hunger she held for him.

"Just this one night," Ethan repeated.

"That's it," she confirmed.

"If that's what you want."

Instead of a verbal response, Zoe placed both hands on either side of his face and pulled him to her. After another passionate kiss, she lifted her shirt over her head. Ethan helped her out of the rest of her clothes and she helped him in the same way.

Fully naked, they admired each other, feeling and touching as if they were handling exquisite works of art. Taking their time, they held each other close, skin to searing skin.

Ethan explored every crevice of her body with adoration, kissing her here and there. She was sure that the moisture from each kiss evaporated immediately from the heat of her body. The more he took his time getting to know her body, the more she wanted to feel him inside of her.

He lifted her from the couch and carried her to the large kitchen island. There, he laid her on her back, kissed and caressed her some more, then buried his face between her thighs and took her into his mouth.

The sensation of his warm tongue made her arch her back, and a moan rose from her core and up her throat. Zoe clawed the smooth surface of the granite countertop, unable to actually grasp anything. She writhed. The pleasure was intense, almost too much to handle but far too good to stop. Her body began convulsing. She grabbed the back of his head, pulled him closer to her. The rhythm of his tongue quickened. She wriggled against his skillful licks, strategic nibbles and powerful sucking as he coaxed the orgasm from her.

Her release was explosive, matching the magnitude of an earthquake, the highest possible rating on the Richter scale. Her back came off the cool countertop, and she heard herself howl. Her muscles clenched, and Ethan cajoled the rest of her climax out of her, suckling and teasing.

She relished the powerful force until she could stand it no longer. She pushed him away, aftershocks rippling through her, and lay in a fetal position until the delectable spasms subsided.

Ethan planted sweet kisses along her side until her body calmed. Then he kissed her, letting Zoe taste herself.

Before she could fully catch her breath, he pulled himself away from her long enough to shield himself with protection. Picking her up from the counter, he carried her to the nearest wall and set her on his erection. Zoe's eyes squeezed shut when he filled her. He grunted beneath her, and she lifted her head to the ceiling with an answering groan. Ethan nibbled at her exposed neck as he plunged in and out of her. Zoe braced against the wall, matching his pace.

She couldn't remember being made love to with such intensity. She opened her eyes; she had to see Ethan in this moment.

He must have felt her looking at him. His eyes opened, and his expression was one of sincere delight. Their gazes locked without breaking their rhythm, hearts pounding, breathing heavy, eyes penetrating. Zoe licked her lips; the deep eye contact intensified the sensations.

She groaned again, helpless, as another climax rose within her, and her head rolled back. She felt herself tighten around him. Ethan moaned and his rhythm quickened.

They moved together, faster and faster, and Zoe's body gave in to the pleasure. Shock waves spread through her, reaching every extremity. She hummed through her release.

Ethan growled, and then his body shook against hers. Wrapping his arms around her, he held on tight as if he would drift away otherwise. They stayed that way with her back against the wall until he was soft enough to slip from her.

Ethan carried her to the bedroom. Gently, he laid her across the bed, climbed in and spooned himself against her back, his arm around her waist. The only noise in the dark room was their breathing slowly returning to a normal pace.

After a while, he asked softly, "Are you okay?"

"I'm fine." Instead of allowing an elephant to join them in the room, Zoe decided to head it off. "Thank you for tonight." She pondered how to express what she was thinking. "I mean, for everything. Thank you for everything… For yesterday and especially tonight." She chuckled. "And please, don't worry. I'm not the clingy type. I knew what I was doing here. I have no expectations. I wanted you just as bad as you wanted me. Monday morning, it will be business as usual. Cool?"

"What if I didn't want business as usual?"

Ethan's words shocked her. She turned to look at his face. He seemed serious. She formed her mouth to respond but nothing came out. For once in her life, Zoe wasn't sure what to say next.

Fourteen

Ethan opened and closed all the cabinets and the refrigerator several times. He and Zoe had eaten most of the snacks. Now they were down to the condiments and the few frozen items left in his freezer, which did him no good this morning. After an unbelievable weekend of constant lovemaking, he was famished and was sure Zoe would wake up feeling the same way.

The last thing on their minds after the first time they'd made love was food. They'd satisfied each other's hunger in more delectable ways.

Finally he pulled half a loaf of bread from the refrigerator along with peanut butter and jelly. He knew Zoe didn't have nut allergies because she often kept some around her office to snack on. He toasted the bread a bit and made both of them sandwiches and then prepared two cups of coffee.

He returned to the bedroom to find the bed empty.

He heard water running in the bathroom sink, so he placed the tray on one of the side tables and walked over to the window to take in the landscape. The view from the bedroom overlooking the East River was by far the best in the entire apartment.

Moments later, he heard the bathroom doorknob click. Zoe emerged, looking sex-worn and gorgeous as hell. She'd attempted to finger-comb her hair into place and was wearing nothing but her panties and one of his T-shirts. He was still in his underwear, as well. He sat on the side of the bed and patted the empty space next to him.

"I made breakfast," he said, pointing to the sandwiches.

"Peanut butter and jelly! How did you know?" Zoe laughed.

"Well, it was all we had left." His own words gave him pause. He'd said *we*. It came out comfortable and familiar, as if they'd been existing as *we* all along.

"Perfect! I love peanut butter and jelly sandwiches."

"Good. Shall we?" he asked. He picked up one plate and handed it to Zoe before taking his own sandwich in his hands.

He turned on the television as they ate. The news updated them on the latest since the storm hit on Friday. It was now Monday and many homes and businesses were still out of power. The bridges and tunnels were back in service, as well as a few subway lines. Others remained shut down due to flooding.

"I can finally get home and assess any damage," Zoe said. "My neighbor has been keeping me posted. The power is back on in some parts of the neighborhood, but it was still hard to get around because so many trees are down. Luckily my mom and sister are okay."

Ethan's phone rang. "Speaking of which. Excuse me, please." He stood and carried his phone conversation to the living room. It was Carter, and Ethan wasn't ready to reveal any details about his weekend with Zoe. "What's up?"

"It's all good," Carter said. "Did you see the email Dad sent? He wants to open up the offices on Wednesday."

"That's good. We have quite a bit of staff affected by the storm. This will give them a little time to get things in order before returning to work," Ethan said. "I'm going to ride out and check out my branches today. I hope we have power. I understand there are lots of trees down across Long Island. It got hit pretty hard. How are your locations?"

"Fortunately not too bad. Power outages are the worst of what we've seen."

"Good."

"You're still in the city?"

"Yeah. Like I said earlier, I'm heading back to Long Island today."

"How's your staff?"

Ethan looked back toward his bedroom. "Fine." He smiled. "I've been in touch with them. Some doing better than others but no major problems overall."

"Good. Mine, too."

Zoe sneezed and Ethan covered his phone, hoping Carter hadn't heard anything. "Okay, big brother," he said. "I'm going to jump in the shower and head to the island. I'll catch up with you later."

"Late start, huh?"

"Uh. Yeah." Ethan didn't offer an explanation. "Call me later?"

"Cool."

Ethan ended the call before Carter could say another word. He returned to the bedroom to find Zoe sitting where he'd left her. It appeared that she was on the phone with her mother. He picked up their empty plates and cups, taking them to the kitchen and giving her privacy for her conversation. He came back when he heard her say goodbye. He was hoping he could make love to her one more time before they both had to leave.

"Hey," he said, leaning on the door frame.

"Hey." She turned to face him and crossed her arms across her chest.

"Can we talk for a second?"

"Sure."

He sat on the bed next to her. "I enjoyed my time with you this weekend and I want you to know that I'd love to continue seeing you. I don't want this to get awkward. We don't have to make it anything serious and we can certainly keep this to ourselves. It was fun. You're fun. We had a good time together."

"Fun is one way of putting it," Zoe said. That made both of them laugh. "I don't want you to feel pressure to make sure that I'm okay. I'm a big girl. We knew what we were doing. We enjoyed it. We don't have to continue something we know can't work."

That stung. Ethan swallowed. He wasn't used to rejection of any kind. But he wasn't ready to let Zoe walk away. He searched his mind for the right words. "I like you. A lot. If I tell the whole truth, I've been attracted to you from the day you stepped foot into my office for your first interview. I've pushed that aside to remain professional, but after this weekend... I realize I don't want this to be over so soon."

Zoe blinked a few times. "Ethan." Her shoulders deflated. "You're my boss... I mean, don't get me wrong.

You're incredibly attractive, which by the way, I noticed from that first interview, as well, but I wouldn't want to jeopardize anything. I like you, too, but I love my job. I don't want to lose it. I don't want to lose the respect of my colleagues. I mean… I—"

Ethan put a hand to her lips. "Let's just have fun. That's all I ask. When it no longer feels like fun, we stop. That's all. Like you said. We're adults. We set the boundaries. We stick to them. We enjoy ourselves in the meantime. And it would be our secret. I would never want to do anything to jeopardize your career or mine anyway." He looked at the crumpled sheets and then back at her. "You're gonna tell me you didn't enjoy yourself this weekend? Can you honestly say you don't want this?" His lips eased into a smirk.

Zoe chuckled, then sighed. "You're so bad, Ethan."

He raised his brow. "You want it?" He felt himself warming for her.

"Ethan! You're making this so hard."

"It doesn't have to be. It will be just between us. When the wheels fall off, we go back to the way things were. We are two mature, consenting adults. So what's it going to be?"

She drew in a long breath. She let it out slowly. Ethan knew the gears were churning inside her head, turning over all the possibilities, both good and bad. He held his breath, awaiting her response.

Zoe groaned. "I'd be lying if I said I didn't want to continue seeing you. I enjoy our time together." Zoe closed her eyes and took a long, slow breath. "I mean I really enjoy being with you. I just—I didn't want any of this to reflect on either of us in a bad way. My career is important to me…" Zoe paused again. She sighed. "Okay. Yes, I want this—"

"Shh." That was all Ethan needed to hear. She wanted this just as much as he did. He vowed to enjoy his time with her as much as possible, knowing that when it was over, their memories would be all they would have to hold on to.

He kissed her, deep, hard and long. Ethan felt his erection rise and he rolled on top of her so she could feel it, too. She slipped her hand into his underwear and massaged him to his fullness.

He moaned but ended their kiss with several soft pecks on her lips, then got up to retrieve protection from the nightstand drawer.

Zoe took it from him, tore it open and slowly rolled it over his erection. Ethan was more rigid than a rock. Climbing over her, he teased her with licks and pecks from her lips to her center until Zoe demanded he enter her. When he did, their eyes rolled back from sheer delight. Together they entertained several positions and rhythms, pleasing one another in all the ways they'd learned from each other in the past forty-eight hours.

Ethan had discovered the ways she liked to be touched and held. By now, he knew how to make her moan. Speaking sweetness in her ear made her moist, and he told her she was beautiful, used soft words to express how she made him feel. She talked back to him. Told him how good he felt to her, inside and out.

Ethan knew when she was getting close to climax. He could feel its ascent, knew how to ride her toward a powerful, body-trembling peak. Since he wasn't sure when he'd get to have her to himself again, he decided to prolong her pleasure.

He slowed his pace—let her catch her breath. Removing himself, he tasted her, bringing her close to that delicious moment with his tongue, and then stopped.

He entered her once more, taking slow, deliberate strokes, trying to give her ultimate bliss while keeping his own excitement at bay. It didn't help. She felt too good.

Grabbing his hips, Zoe pulled him deeper into her. She tightened her walls around his erection until he couldn't stand the pressure anymore. Ethan exploded. So did she. His heart raced, and she panted. His skin tightened, and she held him tight. His muscles spasmed, and she trembled under him. He collapsed. She did, too.

Spent. Happy. Ready for what was next, they lay in each other's arms.

Zoe had become his enchanting little secret. One he would hold on to as long as he could.

Fifteen

Since Zoe returned home, she'd been plowing through an endless list of to-dos. The first was to check in on her mother and sister. Laura had sounded quite tired when they'd spoken on the phone before Zoe left Ethan's house, yet she had insisted that Zoe go and take care of her own home first. Fortunately the power was back on and Zoe wouldn't have to navigate her town house without electricity.

Ethan had taken her home and come inside briefly. The rank smell of her kitchen garbage had been an unpleasant greeting, having sat there since Friday morning and it now being Monday afternoon. Ethan helped her get rid of all the garbage and the spoiled food in her refrigerator. After that, he insisted on helping her with her car, but she convinced him that she would call roadside assistance, so Ethan eventually left.

She spent the rest of her afternoon cleaning her house.

Despite how much she had to do, thoughts of Ethan kept invading her mind.

Despite the severity of the storm, being with him had felt like a vacation—an erotic fantasy lived out loud. Zoe remembered how good he'd made her feel and shivered involuntarily.

That was just it. Ethan was like a fantasy. An indulgent, sensual fantasy. Being with him made her feel like she was starring in a silly romantic comedy or some fairy tale. He was a charming prince—wealthy, worldly and well-rounded. Zoe was the regular girl getting swept off her feet.

But it was so much more than just an opportune moment brought on by being trapped in his apartment. She felt it. Zoe was smitten. Ethan was a man unlike anyone she'd ever dated before. They came from two totally different leagues.

She shook her head as she stacked the last of her bottled waters from her pantry in her fridge. What was she thinking? She couldn't date this man. He was her boss. Why had she agreed to continue seeing him? Now that he wasn't around, she could think more clearly. There was no way she could go through with this.

She thought back to when she'd dated Langston in college. He'd come from a wealthy family just like Ethan's.

One weekend, he'd brought Zoe home to attend a family function. From the moment she'd stepped foot on his family's estate, she'd known she didn't belong. His haughty mother had confirmed that by openly wearing her disdain from the moment she'd said hello. The woman had stared at Zoe through narrowed eyes. Her lips had turned up as if she'd smelled something bad. Both his parents had asked a barrage of questions about her family background. Clearly her modest upbringings hadn't been good enough for their son. Before they'd left, Langston's parents had pulled him aside and denigrated her as if she weren't within earshot.

From that point on, she'd stayed clear of wealthy men. And since she was so protective of her family, she vowed to keep information about them to herself, as well.

She'd have to let Ethan know when he came into her branch this week. She both longed and dreaded to see him.

"Ugh!" she grunted. This was an impossible situation, but she knew what she had to do.

Zoe finished up at home and headed to her mother's house. The moment Laura opened the door, Zoe knew something wasn't right. Laura looked weary, and dark circles framed her eyes.

Concern filled Zoe. "What's wrong, Ma?" She didn't give her time to answer before she made her way into the house. "Where's Shena?" She looked around.

Laura shook her head. "Not in a good place."

Zoe gave her mother a quick kiss on the cheek and went in search of her sister. "Shena," she called.

There was no answer, but she heard feet shuffling over her head.

"Shena." Zoe climbed the stairs frantically, two steps at a time.

Shena was in her bedroom.

"Shena," Zoe called again softly. "Hey. You okay?"

Shena was pacing back and forth, grabbing handfuls of her hair. Tears streamed down her face. Her words were clipped and erratic. She wasn't making sense.

Zoe cautiously stepped into the room. "Wanna talk?"

"No! I don't want to talk to anyone! I can't. I don't

wanna," Shena yelled and went back to her erratic speech.

"Come to my house. I could use your help." Zoe hoped she would agree. Laura needed a break.

Shena stopped pacing. "Why. Who's there?" she snapped.

"It will be just you and me, that's it. I'll make a nice salad. I know how much keeping your figure means to you." Zoe laughed, hoping Shena would, too. "Come on. I could use the company. Please."

Shena sat at the foot of the bed. For several moments, she remained silent. Zoe sighed in relief. Maybe she was going to be okay. Then suddenly, Shena burst into tears.

"Shena." Zoe inched closer and put her arms around her sister's shoulders. "Come with me."

Zoe expected Shena to protest, as she was clearly irritated, but she didn't. "Okay," she said instead in a child-like voice. "I'm so tired." Her voice was weak.

"I know. Pack a bag. We can stop for food along the way." Zoe prayed they'd get to her house without incident. When Shena was in a bad way, her behavior became extreme. At times she was overly giddy; at others she was highly agitated and irrational.

Shena shook her head. While she packed belongings, Zoe went down to tell their mother that she would be taking Shena with her. The Blackwell office was closed for one more day. Zoe didn't mind spending that time helping her mother and sister out. Plus, Shena liked being at Zoe's house. Maybe that could help ease her mood swings. Perhaps she could get to the bottom of what was going on with Shena's meds. With the way she was acting, Zoe was convinced that Shena hadn't been taking them like she said she was.

Once they'd gotten everything together, Zoe asked Shena if she'd packed her medicine.

"No. I don't have anymore. I don't need them anyway."

Zoe wanted to scold her sister, ask her what she was thinking. Instead, she sucked in a deep breath. There was no use going there now. Shena wasn't in the right frame of mind. Zoe knew she'd have to make an appointment, go to the doctor with her sister and make sure she got a new prescription. She'd done it all before.

During the car ride back to Zoe's, Shena said nothing. That gave Zoe space to think, and despite how much was on her mind, Ethan popped up.

She couldn't stop thinking of him. This situation confirmed that continuing to see him wasn't a good idea. What would happen once he got a glimpse into her reality? Would he still be so smitten?

At home, she and Shena ate the food they'd picked up along the way. Shena still said very little. A while later, she lay across the couch and slept like a rock.

Zoe covered her with a throw and headed to her room. In the bathroom, she looked in the mirror. She could see the weariness from lack of rest in her own eyes. She and Ethan hadn't done much sleeping.

And her mind was back on him. Some thoughts made her core flutter, others scared her.

"What. Are. You. Doing?" she said aloud.

This all felt good. In fact it felt amazing and adventurous and forbidden and of course fun, but it had to stop. How long would they be able to hide their affair? Someone was bound to find out. He'd be in major trouble. It would embarrass his family. She'd be out of a job. Plain and simple. Despite how it felt—how she felt—

despite how much fun they had and could potentially have, it was up to Zoe to shut it down.

She decided to tell him when he came to her branch this week. She even went over a few scenarios in her head. She wasn't going to waste any time. The very next time he set foot in her branch, she was going to ask him to her office and explain why they couldn't go on like this.

Zoe arrived at her office extra early on Thursday. Nervous energy coursed through her veins, putting her on edge. Although they'd texted one another, Zoe hadn't laid eyes on Ethan since he had dropped her off at her place on Monday afternoon. A part of her couldn't wait to see his gorgeous face. On the other hand, she just wanted to hurry and speak with him so they could both move on.

Instead of going in on Wednesday, she took an extra day off to visit the doctor's office with Shena to make sure she was set up with the right medicine. She even went to the pharmacy with her to pick up her prescription and made her take the first pill right in front of her. With Shena taken care of without incident, and their mother getting some well-needed rest, there wasn't much left to distract Zoe from thinking of Ethan. And he appeared in her thoughts constantly.

At her desk, she turned on her computer but failed to take in any of the information she scanned in her emails. She sat back and rubbed her temples. "Focus, girl."

She went back to an email from one of the other branch managers who'd had to stay out another day due to home repairs from the storm. She tried to read a few more, but still unable to concentrate, she got up and paced.

She couldn't eject Ethan from her thoughts, so she contemplated the words she would use to let him know they had to end this…this…whatever they were doing before Zoe got hurt.

She practiced letting him down easy, explaining why it made sense to call it quits. She'd even dressed more conservatively than she ever had since she started working at Blackwell: a basic black suit, a black-and-white blouse with a bow at the neck and practical black pumps. "Nothing to see here," she joked, mimicking a police officer.

Zoe's door was closed, but she could hear the chatter of her staff as they arrived for the workday. When Ethan came into the branch, he usually didn't arrive before ten in the morning. She looked at the set of clocks on her wall depicting several time zones. The flat screen on her office wall, always tuned to her favorite financial news network, confirmed that it was just after nine o'clock. She had time.

The moment that thought left her mind she heard his voice.

Her body stiffened. He had arrived.

Three light taps at her door. Instead of answering, Zoe remained still. He tapped again.

"Zoe," Ethan called through the door. His voice went right through her as always.

"One moment." Zoe punched the air twice and huffed. Then she stood tall, straightened her suit jacket and swallowed. She took calculated steps to the door.

"Hey, Ethan," she greeted as if all were cheery. "Come on in. I'm glad you're here early. I need to talk to you." She turned on her heel and headed toward her desk, wringing her hands.

"Cool." Ethan closed the door behind him. She heard the lock click.

Before she could make it to her desk, Ethan caught

up with her, took her by the arm and gently turned her around and kissed her. The kiss was wild and passionate. It felt forbidden.

"Mm. I've missed that," he whispered.

The sweet way he spoke made her knees wobble. Before she could respond, he kissed her again. She welcomed the deep kiss without protest. He pulled her close to him, and Zoe thought she would melt from the heat of their bodies together.

When he softened back, she had to catch her breath. She touched her kiss-swollen lips. Ethan's touch made her weak.

"Ethan." She found her voice, scolding him with the way she said his name.

"Don't worry, I locked your door." He planted a series of pecks on her lips before letting her go. He sat in the chair across from her desk.

Zoe needed a few seconds to gather herself. This wasn't going as she'd planned. Finally she sat. "Ethan," she said evenly.

"Wait!" He held his hand up. "Do you know who Leah Cartwright is? What do you think about her?"

"Of course I know who she is. I think she's amazing. Why?"

"Good. Would you like to meet her?"

"Wait. What?" Zoe was confused. "What are you talking about, Ethan?"

"I thought you would. She's coming to the Barclays this weekend to speak and sign her new book. A friend dropped some VIP tickets in my lap. We can meet her backstage after the event."

Zoe's mouth dropped. She admired Leah Cartwright immensely. She had never been the fangirl type but Leah Cartwright was…different. She was Zoe's favorite motivational speaker. Zoe had watched her talk show when it was still on the air and had read all of her books. She'd always wanted to attend one of Leah's live appearances. When she'd heard that Leah was coming to New York, she'd wanted to attend but the tickets had cost hundreds of dollars. As much as Zoe loved Leah, she wasn't willing to sell off stock to see her.

But what Ethan had offered was different. Not only would Zoe get to see her, she would be able to actually meet her. She was going to meet Leah Cartwright in the flesh!

"Wait!" Zoe held her hand up. She couldn't let Ethan suck her in. She had to put a stop to this. "Ethan."

"What's wrong? I thought you'd like this. The opportunity came up and I thought of you, but if you don't want to go, it's fine. I'd still like to spend time with you this weekend. I have a few great places that I'd like to take you. All off the beaten path."

Zoe sighed. She wanted to spend time with him both on and off the beaten path. That was the truth.

She really liked him. What if she truly fell for him and all of a sudden, they had to end it all? By then she'd be in too deep. It would hurt more later. If she cut ties now, she could put the weekend behind her and accept the fact that they would never be together.

But just like him, she really wanted more. Zoe closed her eyes and shook her head.

"Zoe?" Ethan looked concerned.

"What are we getting into here, Ethan?"

"Just having fun, remember? But I don't want to push you." The light in his eyes dimmed a little. "Think about the event this weekend. Let me know. Okay?"

Zoe watched him walk out of her office. She dropped her head into her hands and groaned.

Sixteen

Ethan was happy to get the call from Zoe about the Leah Cartwright event. There was something about Zoe; he didn't understand it himself, but he wasn't willing to just let it pass. Being with her felt good, even though he knew it was wrong.

He'd managed to keep his weekend with Zoe to himself so far and planned to keep things that way. That could present a problem down the line, but he wanted to see how far this could go. As long as he was careful, they would be fine.

Ethan's driver maneuvered along the streets of Zoe's neighborhood with ease now, but he knew that once they hit downtown Brooklyn, traffic would be a nightmare. He didn't feel like being bothered with congested streets and lack of parking, so he'd ordered a car to take them to the event and bring them back. First, they would have dinner at a friend's restaurant near Dumbo. It was an exclusive place off the beaten path. Ethan wasn't worried about running into Carter. He had called him earlier in the day to gauge his whereabouts for the evening.

The driver pulled up in front of Zoe's town house. Ethan stepped out, straightened his suit and walked to her door. After a few quick taps, the door opened, and Zoe filled the entrance with her gorgeous frame. She looked radiant in a touch more makeup than she normally wore to the office. Her hot pink lips were enticing. Her electric blue jumpsuit was stylish and the pink shoes and handbag finished her look in that well-put-together, unexpected way she always managed.

Ethan felt himself smile. "You look amazing."

"Thank you. Let me get my jacket."

Zoe went back in, grabbed her coat and met him back at the door in no time. He reached for her hand as they walked to the car. She looked around and hesitated before placing her hand in his.

"There's no one around here we need to worry about," he said, realizing she was nervous. Prior to this, they had spent all their time together indoors.

"I guess." She shrugged.

Ethan stopped walking and faced her. "Thanks for coming. I'm glad you changed your mind. I promise this will be fun, and like I said, as soon as we're no longer having fun, we'll stop. No hard feelings."

"Ethan." Zoe paused. "What if the fun doesn't stop or we end up taking things further?"

"Yeah."

They stared at one another. Silence blossomed between them for a few long moments.

"We'll cross that bridge when we get there. Okay?" Ethan finally said. "We'll just shift our focus back to work. It will be our secret. No hard feelings. How hard could that be for two consenting adults?"

Zoe pressed her lips together. "Okay." She shook her head as if she needed to confirm what her mouth had just said with an action.

"But let's not think about that now. Let's just focus on the fun part."

Zoe nodded. "Okay," she said again.

"All in?" Ethan asked.

"All in," she replied.

At the exquisite French restaurant, Ethan greeted his friend Jacques. The host led them to a table overlooking the water.

"I forgot to ask," Ethan said to Zoe. "How's your family after the storm? Did they suffer any flooding or damage?"

He noticed that she looked away. A moment ticked by before she answered. "Fortunately—" she picked up her wineglass and sipped "—they're fine. No floods. No outages."

"Are you all close?"

"Yes. We're a small bunch."

Ethan changed the subject. Zoe didn't seem enthusiastic about that conversation. The waiter returned with their appetizers.

"Ready to order your entrées or would you like a little more time?" The waiter's French accent stitched his words together like a melody. Ethan smiled and listened carefully as Zoe placed her order. He wanted to know all about the things she liked.

"Ever been to Paris?" he asked her once the waiter left.

"No, but I like his accent." Her spirits seemed to lift, evidently liking this conversation better than the one about family. "It's on my bucket list. I want to set foot on the other six continents."

"I see. Which ones haven't you been to?"

"Outside of North America, I've only traveled to islands off the coast of South America. How many continents have you traveled to?"

"All but Antarctica."

"If I were to leave one out, that would be the one. It's probably too cold for my blood." Zoe laughed.

Ethan smiled. He liked the sound of her laugh. "What other areas are on your bucket list?"

"Just about everywhere," she admitted gamely. "London, Iceland, Scotland, Paris, Ethiopia, Italy, Greece, Tokyo, South Africa, Australia. You're going to have to pay me more money so I can get to some of these places."

"Ha!" Ethan leaned forward over the table. "I see where your bonus is going. If we win this competition with the other branches, we'll both have more to travel with."

"Speaking of which… I know we're not supposed to talk about work, but I have this great idea of doing a series of information sessions that I think will be helpful for current and prospective clients and it could also help bring in more business."

"Really?" He drew back. "Tell me more."

Zoe explained her idea in more detail. Ethan simply shook his head while she explained.

"Wow! That's brilliant."

"I believe it will set us apart from competitors both inside and outside of the company and show how we place a strong focus on service and value. The industry has changed so much." Zoe took a sip of her wine. "Lost that personal touch. I think people would like that."

Ethan pondered her idea. "I love it. Let's get started on that first thing Monday. Outline what these events would look like. We can get on a management call with the rest of the team and begin rolling these out branch by branch across our territory and see how it works."

"Don't tell Carter," she warned. "If this works, it will give us an advantage over the other regions and we'll win for sure."

"I like your thinking, Zoe."

They talked more over dinner about ways to boost business, each idea giving them more energy. He loved how passionate she was about business. Zoe constantly confirmed her worth. He'd picked the best.

But as much as he loved talking shop with her, he eventually turned the conversation back to the two of them. They could talk about business Monday through Friday from nine to five. This time he had with her tonight was personal. That was what Ethan wanted for this night—to get personal with Zoe.

Their dinner was as delectable as Ethan had anticipated. The moment they finished, he paid the bill, gave the waiter a hefty tip and together, he and Zoe jumped back into their waiting car and headed over to the Barclays. Ethan held her hand in the car. He wanted to do much more than that but kept his cool. Memories of the explosive times they'd shared in his bed invaded his thoughts. There was more to Zoe than great sex and he wanted to explore those things, too.

When they arrived, he helped her out of the car but purposely let go of her hand as they walked past the long, winding lines leading up to the main entrance and headed over to the VIP doorway. They were greeted politely and ushered right inside. Zoe kept a cool expression on her face, but he could tell she was excited.

Inside the suite, Ethan greeted his colleague Colin, a tall, muscular, bald gentleman with stark blue eyes. He pulled Ethan into a bear hug as his greeting.

"Colin, this is Zoe Baldwin," Ethan introduced them. "She runs the Garden City branch of Blackwell Wealth Management."

"It's great to meet you, Zoe." Colin offered her a firm handshake.

"It's great to meet you, too, Colin. Thanks for the invitation."

"Anytime." He patted the back of Ethan's shoulder with his large hand and repeated, "Anytime," with a warm smile. "We've got food, drinks, everything. Enjoy yourselves, and when this is all over, we'll go down and meet Mrs. Cartwright. Cool?"

"Cool," Ethan and Zoe said simultaneously.

Ethan watched Zoe look around at the impressive spread inside the suite. Gourmet finger foods lined one side of the suite. On the other side was an array of salads, crudités, desserts and wine and liquor. Inside a stainless steel refrigerator were more beverages of every kind. Ethan and Zoe ate, drank and mingled with the few other people Colin had invited to his suite until the program started.

When Leah Cartwright sauntered onstage, Zoe gave the revered speaker her undivided attention. Minutes into the presentation, it seemed like the only two people in the room were Zoe and Leah. Ethan watched Zoe's starry eyes as she took in every word that fell from Leah's mouth.

At the end, Zoe sighed. Ethan wondered if she had held her breath the entire hour and a half.

"I need a drink." Those were the first words that Zoe had spoken since the show started.

Ethan looked at her bright, excited eyes and chuckled. "You okay?"

"That was amazing. She's amazing. I need a drink so I can calm down a bit before meeting her." Zoe laughed at herself.

"At your service." He waved an arm like a server. "What would you like?"

"More red wine would be great."

"Be right back." He returned a few short moments later with two glasses of wine and sat back beside her. "I believe you enjoyed it, so tell me what you thought about it."

"Goodness!" Zoe shook her head as if trying to think of the right words. "She's so…so…real. Yeah. So real and down to earth. Like we could be friends. I could literally see sitting down and having dinner with her. She's brilliant. Just… This was incredible. Thanks again, Ethan."

"Yeah, she's pretty brilliant."

"And those boots! Woo. I need to find those. I mean, I probably can't afford them, but that wouldn't stop me from trying them on." Zoe laughed.

Ethan thought about finding those boots for her. Wondered if they would make her smile just as brightly as she did now.

"Everybody cool?" Colin's voice boomed through the suite.

A few yeses rang out. Others nodded their heads.

"Then let's go meet our guest of honor."

Ethan took Zoe by the hand and they followed Colin and their private escort to what looked like a lounge behind the scenes of the arena. Ethan watched Zoe's face as she scanned the room in search of Leah Cartwright and smiled deep in his core when Zoe's mouth dropped at the site of her. She closed it quickly enough.

Leah greeted everyone and thanked them all for coming. After a few sips of water, she took her place in front of a step-and-repeat and held brief conversations with people as she shook hands and took pictures.

When it was Zoe's turn, Ethan stepped aside so she could chat with Mrs. Cartwright. Their photographer took a few shots, then Zoe had Ethan take some with her phone. She waved him over to join in, but he politely declined. He would have loved to share in the moment but thought it was best that he avoid taking pictures at this juncture. Besides, he wanted to let Zoe fully enjoy her moment.

Leah and Zoe ended their brief time together with a few selfies. Leah wrapped Zoe in a gracious hug, sending her off with a smile that spread halfway around her face.

"This was amazing. I will never forget this day. Thanks again, Ethan."

"We have Colin to thank."

"You're right. But you could have brought anyone here with you tonight. You chose me. So...thank you." Zoe planted a sweet peck on his cheek. Despite the gesture seeming more friendly than sensual, a spark ignited in Ethan's belly.

The kiss awakened his desire for her. Simple touches from her made him weak. All evening, they had been careful to avoid any telling touches. But now she'd unleashed the passion he'd tried to keep behind his polished exterior. The air in the room seemed to have become warmer. He looked around to see if anyone was paying attention. No one appeared to notice.

"Ready to go?" he asked.

Her seductive gaze was sweltering. "Sure." It seemed that the same desire awakening in him was also awakening in her.

Ethan said a quick thank-you to Colin and called for the driver to meet them at the VIP access entrance. They entered the car as hastily as they had said their goodbyes. For the first few seconds, they stared at each other, and then broke out into laughter.

Their desire was now palpable, pulsing in the air like a heartbeat. Ethan held out his hand. Somehow, knowingly, Zoe reached for it and laced her fingers between his.

Ethan made sure the partition in the limo was up before pulling her toward him and capturing her mouth with his. Their hands explored one another's bodies, and they kissed themselves breathless, touching, caressing, roaming and grasping each other. Ethan felt himself grow rigid in his pants. He pulled away from her just long enough to catch his breath before going back for more. Her lips tasted like heaven. Her mouth felt like clouds. He wanted to be inside of her.

Totally unaware of how much time had passed, Ethan pulled himself away from Zoe and looked through the window when he felt the car roll to a stop. They had arrived at her complex. He huffed, trying to contain the sexual tension pent up inside of him. He didn't want the night to end but that would have to be Zoe's choice.

"You coming...inside?" she asked.

Ethan licked his lips instinctively. He didn't miss the innuendo. "As long as you want me to."

"Oh. I want you to."

Ethan didn't wait for the driver to exit the car and come around to the door. Instead, he shot out and was at Zoe's door in an instant.

"No worries, man." Ethan waved his hand. "I'm good. I'll call for a pickup when I'm ready. Thanks!" He took Zoe by the hand and the two made quick steps to her front door.

Inside her town house, their lips connected again. Zoe kicked the door closed with her foot, and Ethan turned the locks. Their lips never parted. She tugged at his shirt. He undid the buttons and she peeled it off his shoulders. Ethan unzipped her jumpsuit, sliding his fingers into her sleeves to maneuver it down her body. She stepped out of the outfit and removed his belt. Tearing, peeling and pulling, they relieved each other of their clothes and left them pooled at their feet.

Ethan stepped back, putting a few inches of space between them. His breath was ragged. He craved her but needed to admire her natural beauty. He took her in, feasting on her visually from head to toe. Zoe's body was magnificent—flawless to him. Maybe he was blinded by her beauty, but every time he had the honor of seeing her in her natural glory, he felt the same way. Even her imperfections were perfect.

Zoe looked at him in a similar way. He watched her gaze rake over him ravenously, then she reached one hand behind his neck and wrapped her other hand around his erection. She pulled him toward her, and Ethan went willingly.

Their kiss was wild, unbridled and hungry. He embraced her firmly and lifted her up off the floor. He carried her to the dining table, moved her stylish place settings out of the way and laid her down.

Zoe groaned before he even touched her body again. He trailed her sweet caramel skin with kisses from her lips to her knees. Zoe reached for him—he'd grown as rigid as stone—and guided him inside of her, forgoing the tease and getting straight to the point. A sound caught in her throat for the first of countless times that weekend.

Ethan didn't make it home that night.

Or the next.

Seventeen

Ethan hadn't, as they say, rocked Zoe's world. He'd completely shifted her universe. She couldn't get enough of him. And he tried his best to give Zoe her fill. She'd spent so much time with him in recent weeks that she felt guilty about not spending as much time with her family.

This week, she'd taken some time off to be with her mother and sister. They were a trying few days, ending with Zoe taking Shena for a follow-up visit with her doctor. Zoe looked forward to Shena bouncing back from a manic high. One of the days had been so bad that Zoe had waited half the night for Shena to experience a moment where she could get through to her. Shena had cursed her sister, but Zoe had remained calm. She was committed to working with Shena through her ups and downs and holding her hand through it all.

Being away from work meant being away from Ethan. She communicated with him mostly by text when she was with her family. She missed him horribly. At management meetings or during his visits to her office, they avoided each other. Outside of work, they spent every night and weekend they possibly could together.

He stimulated every part of Zoe: her mind, her body, her heart... She had never dated a man like Ethan before. Her body had never hungered for a man's touch the way hers did for Ethan's. The sound of his lowered voice was enough to make her moist.

She chalked it all up to the forbidden nature of their relationship. That, she assumed, was what made their trysts so exciting.

They graduated from weekends in bed to exclusive romantic experiences, like when Ethan had a famous chef friend prepare an incredible meal at his restaurant on the only night they were closed. Most people had to wait weeks to get a reservation at that place, but they'd had the entire restaurant to themselves on a Monday night. After their meal, they'd danced to a playlist on Ethan's phone, then gone home and made love until dawn. Zoe had been giddy and exhausted the next morning at work.

She wished their "fun" could last forever. She hoped no one would become suspicious. Either way, she was going to enjoy as much of Ethan as possible for as long as she could. Hopefully it wouldn't hurt too much when they got to a point where it all had to end. If she were honest, she'd admit how much she cared about him. But being truthful about her feelings would never be enough.

Still, they grew closer in other ways, too. Being with Ethan so much, she realized how important it was for him to please his father. He worked harder than his brothers, but never seemed to feel like he could ever do enough. But as much as they talked, she never revealed the complete truth about her background or her sister's mental illness. Her life was such a contrast to Ethan's affluent, near-perfect lifestyle. How could they ever bring those two worlds together?

Zoe's cell phone rang at work, startling her. The sound pulled her focus from her inner thoughts. She'd almost forgotten where she was. She picked the phone up from her desk, tapped a key on her computer to bring it to life and said, "Hello."

"Hey." Ethan's voice made her heartbeat quicken.

"Hey, yourself."

"How's your mom doing?"

"Fine. Everyone is just fine," she said, feeling a bit guilty for the white lie she'd told him about her prior absence from work. Instead of telling him about her sister's episode, she'd said her mother wasn't feeling well and she needed to accompany her to a few doctor's appointments.

"That's good. I miss you."

Zoe looked around her office. The door was closed, and she was alone. No one could possibly hear Ethan on her phone. Overcautious. She chuckled at herself. "I miss you, too."

"If you'll let me, I'd like to take you on a little excursion. I want to show you a good time. Actually, I want to show you how much I miss you."

Zoe giggled. She wasn't sure how she'd allowed Ethan to reduce her to a giggling little girl. "Where?"

"It's a surprise."

"Okay, then. When?"

"Take off tonight. I'll pick you up this evening and have you back home by Sunday night."

She shook her head with a smile. "You're impossible. Where are we going?"

"Just somewhere to spend some time together. I'll help you pack to make sure you're dressed right."

"What?"

"Are you in?"

Zoe laughed, placed her elbow on her desk and her hand on her forehead. "Yes. I'm in."

"I'll be at your house at six sharp." He ended the call.

She looked at her phone and then at her computer screen. It would be six more hours before she got to see Ethan's handsome face, and she couldn't wait.

She took a deep breath. Ethan had stolen her focus and filled her with anticipation. How would she get through the rest of the day? She needed to concentrate in order to finish preparing for the next few information sessions. The idea she'd come up with a few weeks back while out with Ethan had proved to be extremely profitable. They'd held three reception-like sessions so far, offering clients and guests wine and refreshments. The results had been more solid relationships with existing clients and additional accounts with new clients.

Zoe took a quick break to clear her head, returned to her desk and got back to work. The second the clock turned to five, she was out the door. At six, she was on her couch, waiting for Ethan with a drink in one hand for her and another on the table for him. As always, he was right on time.

He knocked and she opened the door right away, handing him his drink. They kissed in between a few sips, then Ethan put his glass down and took her by the hand. Zoe followed his lead. Moments later they were in bed, showing each other how much they had missed one another. Afterward, they both collapsed in each other's arms, unable to move. She stayed put until the waves of pleasure rolling through her body subsided.

"We have to go!" Ethan groaned. Lazily, he pushed the tangled sheets aside and climbed out of bed. Reaching for Zoe, who shot him a puzzled look, he said, "Come on."

She groaned. Although she'd rather stay in bed, she peeled herself from the comfort of the cozy mattress. He grabbed her hand and led her to the shower. They made love there again but quickly.

Back in her room, he told her to pull out a suitcase and asked her to pack enough outfits for that night through to Sunday. Zoe was confused when he said to make sure she added a warm coat, scarf, gloves, boots and bathing suits to the bag.

An hour later, they were in a waiting room at JFK airport, preparing to board a private plane.

Zoe had never experienced anything like this before. There was coffee, refreshments and cushioned chairs in the waiting area. It was nothing like the crowds and hard plastic seats of the regular terminal.

Ethan held her hand as they cuddled in the comfortable seats. It was so different than when they went out locally, acting as if there were regular friends or work colleagues. She enjoyed being in his arms in public. She allowed herself to relax and take in yet another incredible experience at the hands of Ethan Blackwell. She could get used to letting a man take the lead and was surprised to realize that she trusted him enough to do so.

Zoe didn't realize she'd fallen asleep on his shoulder until he nudged her awake.

"It's time to go."

She followed Ethan along a pristine Jetway onto an airplane with a creamy-beige interior and cushioned leather couches along the walls. A few chairs faced one another at each end of the jet, with polished wood tables nestled between them. Their flight attendant greeted them with a warm smile, letting them know they could sit anywhere they wanted.

Ethan sat on one of the couches, pulling Zoe down beside him. Their attendant offered them drinks, brought them promptly, then disappeared behind one of the cream-colored walls.

Minutes later, Zoe could feel the plane taking off. Ethan put on soft music and sat back beside her.

"Now will you tell me where we're going?" she asked.

"One of the places on your bucket list."

Zoe sat up. "Are you kidding me?" She tried to think back to all the places she'd told him she wanted to visit. "Which one?"

"The closest one. Now get some rest. There won't be much sleeping after we land."

All she could do was shake her head in disbelief. At last, she rested on his shoulder again. What if she could be with Ethan forever?

"Welcome to Iceland."

Zoe squeezed her eyes, blinked and opened them slowly.

"We're here," she heard Ethan say.

Where was here? She had to get her bearings. Yawning, she recalled the airport terminal and getting on the plane with Ethan. Slowly she began to rise from the sofa. "I thought I was dreaming."

Ethan laughed. "That's a good thing. It's time to get off this bird."

She stood and stretched. Whatever he had planned, she was ready for it. These memories would be hers to cherish far beyond their time together. Thinking of the experiences they shared in this way made the inevitable end much less distressing.

Ethan had a car waiting for them outside.

"Are we really in Iceland?" Zoe had to confirm.

"Yep."

"Oh, my goodness, Ethan!"

"You said you wanted to visit. It was only a five-hour flight. Much closer than all the other places you mentioned. And close enough for a nice weekend getaway."

"And the flight."

"Courtesy of a friend. He owed me."

"Wow!" Zoe got in the car, a cushy luxury ride. She held Ethan's hand but stared out the window. There wasn't much to see this early in the morning, but she was too excited to turn away. She wanted to see everything possible. "Is this your first time here?" she asked.

"No but it will probably be my best."

"Why is that?"

"Because I'm here with you," Ethan said evenly.

Zoe pressed her lips together. "You're trying to butter me up."

"I'm serious."

She looked at him suspiciously. He didn't crack a smile. He seemed serious enough. She looked back out the window.

The four-star hotel was the epitome of luxury. After a quick check-in, they entered their room to find a space that rivaled the size of her entire town house. Clean lines, simple but elegant decor and large windows offered a plush and inviting feel. Zoe marveled at the view of the water below them and what appeared to be snow-capped mountains in the distance.

"What body of water is that?"

"It's the Blue Lagoon."

"Wait! What?" Zoe's eyes widened. "Seriously?"

"Yep. Hungry?"

"Ethan!" He was too nonchalant about all of this. Zoe wanted to burst into tiny little pieces with excitement. "Is that really the Blue Lagoon?" She pressed her forehead against the window. "Oh, my goodness. You have to be kidding me. I'm in Iceland. At a hotel. Overlooking the freaking Blue Lagoon and you're sitting here like we're in your apartment above the muddy East River. Ethan! This is incredible!" She leaped toward him seated on the couch, straddled him and planted kisses all over his face.

Ethan laughed.

"I can't believe you," she said at last.

"I love seeing you smile."

Zoe stared into his eyes. They seemed to sparkle. She kissed him again, this time on his lips. Passion rose inside of her. She was about to make love to Ethan Blackwell, in a room big enough to fit her entire town house, as they looked over the milky-blue water.

Ethan made love to her with care, with the beauty of the lagoon beckoning them through the bedroom window. Zoe woke a few hours later feeling like she was still living inside of a dream.

"Put your bathing suit on underneath your clothes but dress warm," Ethan instructed.

"Whatever you say, buddy." She was giddy again. She couldn't help it when he did things like this. Being with him felt like Christmas came at will. "Where is this journey starting?"

"The Secret Lagoon."

Zoe had never heard of the Secret Lagoon but squealed anyway. She did as he said and put on a bikini under her jeans, sweater and coat.

A shuttle picked them up at the hotel for some sight-seeing before going to the lagoon. It drove them through some of the most breathtaking landscapes she'd ever seen in her life.

Zoe was amazed at how cool the weather was, but the lagoon was nonetheless hot and steamy. They stripped down to their swimwear.

Ethan stepped into the water and dunked his body until only his neck was above the water. Zoe took her time savoring the moment. Who knew if she'd ever have a chance like this again? She stepped in, one foot at a time. The sensation sent a cozy feeling over her. She put the other foot in and moaned. Slowly she descended deeper into the sultry water.

The cool weather had nothing on the warmth that wrapped around her as she dipped her body lower. It was like she had cloaked herself with a heated blanket.

Ethan watched her, waiting. She swam to him and kissed his lips, and he lay back to float, pulling her with him. The two frolicked in the hot spring like kids at a neighborhood pool. They swam, waded, soaked and floated for the better part of an hour. Zoe's stomach growled and she realized it had been quite a while since they'd eaten.

"Hungry?" she asked Ethan.

"Depends on what you're asking if I'm hungry for."

Zoe swatted at him playfully. "Naughty boy. That can be dessert. Right now, I need food."

Ethan led her out of the lagoon, and they dressed and ate at the nearby café. She fed him off her plate, and he licked her fingers seductively.

They moved on to the next part of their excursion, touring a volcano. Their weekend continued at that pace, a whirlwind of nonstop tours and activities. The only downtime they had was overnight, which they spent much of making love. By the time they got back to New York Sunday night, she and Ethan were exhausted. That didn't stop them from making love well into the night and falling asleep in each other's arms once more.

It was past midnight when Ethan rose to head home. Zoe didn't want him to leave. She knew his schedule for the week, and it was a hectic one; she wouldn't get to see him again until the managers' meeting in Manhattan on Thursday.

He said goodbye with a deep, passionate kiss. "Get some rest," he said before walking out the door.

Zoe missed him immediately. The void of his absence loomed over the bedroom.

She felt like she was living a real-life fantasy, but that wasn't what this was at all. This was a secret. Some would call it a dirty little secret. Zoe was having an affair with her boss. It was the stuff of scandalous television shows and novels. Some days it felt fun, mysterious and exciting. Others, like now, it felt…unfair. A part of her knew this could never be her real life. There was too much at stake. She could lose her job. Her income supported her family. Her mother would be so disappointed. What would her colleagues think of her? They'd lose respect for her. Despite all of that, the idea of their affair coming to an end was what she dreaded most.

Truth be told, Zoe cared for Ethan—deeply. She'd fallen deeper than she'd ever expected. There was so much to adore about him. He was witty, kind, intelligent and savvy. She loved how he commanded the attention of a room full of people. And yes, he was handsome beyond explanation with the taut body of an athlete. He knew how to have fun and most of all, he was considerate. Ethan listened to her, sifted through her words and held on to what he knew was important.

She hadn't realized how much that meant to her until now. She'd never dated a man as considerate as him before. In fact, she'd never dated a man like him at all.

Zoe didn't dare think that she loved Ethan just yet, but she could easily see herself falling in love with him if they didn't put an end to this soon. Either that or they'd get caught.

Which would be worse?

Eighteen

"You're coming to the management meeting, right?" Carter asked.

"Of course. Why would you ask that?" Carter's comment caught Ethan off guard.

"You've been MIA a lot lately. I've barely gotten to speak to you. What's going on?"

"With me? Nothing. Just been busy."

"Busy with Zoe?" Carter asked. Accusation rang in his voice.

Ethan almost hit the brakes in the middle of the parkway. He tried to recover quickly and make sure his pause didn't last too long. "Why would you ask that?"

"Come on, bro. This is me. I know when something's up. You haven't been around. I stopped by your house last Saturday and your car was there, but you weren't. It was pretty late. I wanted to crash there after hanging out with this new lady. I called, you didn't answer and you didn't call me back until the next day. When you do get on the phone, you don't have much time to talk unless it's during the workday. I tried to get you a few times this weekend and your phone went straight to voice mail."

"What makes you think that has anything to do with Zoe?"

"From what I see… I think you're hooked. You're not hiding this well, bro."

"Don't be ridiculous, Carter. I know what I'm doing. Don't worry about me."

"If that's the case, why did Dad ask me about you and her after the last management meeting?"

Ethan's eyes widened. It felt like a brick fell in the pit of his stomach. "What?"

"Don't worry. I covered for you. I assured him that everything was good."

"Shit!"

"Just be careful. And listen, you don't have to hide anything from me. I've got your back."

"Thanks, Carter. I'll see you at the meeting."

Ethan felt like turning the car around, but it was too late. He had already reached Zoe's exit. They'd planned on riding into the city together for the meeting. Now he felt like that wasn't such a good idea. They definitely shouldn't come back together. He'd tell Zoe he needed to stay in Manhattan for more meetings and send her back by herself so they wouldn't be seen leaving together.

What had made his father ask Carter about them? Had Ethan done or said something that caused suspicion? He and Zoe had promised to enjoy one another until the fun stopped. And after his conversation with Carter, Ethan felt like the fun was suddenly coming to an abrupt end. He tried to think of anything that he'd done to raise suspicion. He and Zoe couldn't keep their hands off each other in private, but in public they were very careful—especially at work.

He pulled up in front of her house with a thousand questions trampling through his mind. He got out of his car and Zoe met him at her door as usual, yanking him inside by his tie. She wrapped her arms and legs around him and kissed his lips.

"I missed you." She planted pecks all over his face.

"I missed you, too." He couldn't keep the stress out of his voice.

Zoe stopped kissing him and studied his face. "What's wrong?" She put her feet back on the ground.

"Just work stress."

"Aren't we in the lead? The information sessions have been great for business."

"That's fine, but it's other stuff. Carter, Dillon and I have to meet with my dad after our management meeting this morning." Telling that lie stung. A knot tightened in the center of his chest. He hated not being truthful with Zoe.

"Oh. Poor baby. Just come back here after work and I'll help you feel better." She kissed him again.

"Yeah. I'll do that." He needed time to think. "Let's get going."

"Okay. Let me get my stuff." Zoe grabbed her keys and purse. Her cheerful demeanor was a stark contrast to Ethan's unsettled mood.

He forced a smile, trying to push back the stress taking over his mind. The ride to the city was mostly quiet. Giving him space for his mood, Zoe didn't speak much. Ethan appreciated that. Instead she focused on her phone, bobbed to the music on the radio and watched the city passing through her passenger window.

He felt bad for dampening their time together with his anxiety. He looked over at her staring out the window and took her by the hand. He didn't say anything, just held her hand. She squeezed his in return. He was grateful she didn't press him to talk because he needed time to find the right words to say.

The meeting began in its usual fashion; the team chatted over coffee, bagels, yogurt and fruit. Bill called everything to order and they went over the numbers for each territory. Ethan's team had a strong lead and they'd already planned to share their newest tactic for building the business with the rest of the branches.

All eyes were on Zoe as she spoke about the information sessions held by each branch in their region and the impact on business as a result.

"…and the feedback from our clients was overwhelmingly positive," she went on. "We asked them to complete surveys at the end of the sessions and via email. They all seemed to appreciate the face time with the advisors as well as the opportunity to network with other clients. They were happy to have been able to invite guests—many of whom became clients," she pointed out. "They also liked having a forum to learn about additional investment options and hear from guest speakers such as attorneys and tax professionals who were able to provide additional insight into their investment choices." She swept her gaze around the room confidently. "Overall, it's been a huge success with direct results to the bottom line for all of our branches. Oh, and something they all seemed to agree on is that we serve great food and wine."

Everyone chuckled and Zoe looked over to Jasmine, who picked up where she left off.

"A few even suggested a few good wines for upcoming sessions. Here's what else we learned..." Jasmine went on to speak about challenges that they were working through, such as the best methods for following up, obtaining feedback and determining the best days of the week to host the sessions.

Ethan was proud of his team. It was important for him to have the branch managers do the reporting for this initiative so they could get the spotlight. He was especially proud of Zoe, since this had been her innovative idea. He found himself staring at her as he thought of how much of an asset she'd become to the company.

When he glanced over at Carter, his brother was already staring at him. Carter discreetly raised a brow. Ethan sat back and sighed quietly.

He wanted the meeting to be over so he could think. Too many things swirled in his mind, making it hard to concentrate. He felt Carter looking at him and thought he felt his father's eyes on him, too.

Ethan was thinking too hard and making something out of nothing.

When the meeting finally ended, Ethan was ready to go. He'd almost forgotten about the lie he'd told Zoe earlier about meeting with Dillon, Carter and his dad. Like always, the meeting disbanded and the branch managers split off to chat. They had begun to bond and these meetings were the only times they really got to see one another at work. A group of them decided to get together for lunch before heading back to their respective offices.

Ethan stayed behind with Carter and his father. Dillon headed back to Westchester for a meeting with a big prospective client.

"Ethan. Can I talk to you?" Bill asked.

Ethan stilled at the sound of his father's voice. He swallowed hard and turned around. "Sure, Dad. What's up?"

"Carter. Give us a minute, please."

"No problem, Dad. Ethan, let me know when you're heading out so we can handle that."

"Yeah. Will do," Ethan replied. He and Carter had nothing to handle. That was code for *we'll talk after this*. If Bill wanted to speak with Ethan about anything that had to do with Zoe, he was going to need to talk to his brother afterward.

Carter left and Bill pointed to the chair next to the one he sat in at the head of the conference table. "Have a seat, son."

Bill's tone made Ethan's stomach clench. He sat down more slowly than usual and folded his hands on the table to keep them still.

"Is everything okay over in Long Island?" Bill asked at last.

"Of course. We're doing great! You heard our reports. I'm excited."

"That's not what I'm concerned about."

Ethan held his sigh. "What are you concerned about, Dad?"

"You and Zoe. Is there something going on between the two of you?"

Ethan felt the seconds ticking between his father's question and his answer. He wasn't a liar and he didn't want to add another lie to the ones he'd already told today.

It obviously took him too long to answer.

"Ethan." The disappointment in the way Bill said his name made Ethan pull in his bottom lip. He began gnawing on it. "We discussed this! You know how I feel about this kind of thing. We have strict policies in place for good reason. Blackwell can't afford to take another hit on our name if your little fling with this woman goes south. Do you remember the scrutiny we faced?" Bill sat back and huffed, slamming his hand against the table. "You're the last person in this company I would expect to have this conversation with. Twice! Are you willing to jeopardize everything? Even your title?" Bill stood.

His words stung but Ethan kept his gaze forward, refusing to look down.

Bill paced a moment and plopped back down in his chair. "She's not worth it! She's not even on your level." Those words made Ethan's jaw twitch. "You need to end this immediately."

"Um… I'm sorry."

Ethan and Bill turned abruptly at the sound of Zoe's voice.

"Please excuse my interruption," she said. "I left my files on the table."

From the change in her tone, Ethan knew she'd heard some of what his father had just said.

"Sure." Bill waved her in. "Come on in and get it." His smile seemed genuine enough, but Ethan knew his father. "Great presentation today."

"Thank you," Zoe said dryly. She cleared her throat and briskly walked to where she'd been sitting during the meeting, snatched her folder and headed out of the conference room just as fast. "Enjoy the rest of your day," she said without looking at either one of them.

Once she was gone, Ethan released the breath he'd been holding.

"I expect that you will handle this accordingly." Bill stood again. This time he pulled his suit jacket together, signaling the end of this encounter.

"I understand. I wouldn't put the company in any jeopardy. Our reputation matters to me, as well." Ethan paused to contemplate his next comment. "Zoe is an exceptional employee and an amazing woman. She'd be a great fit for any man who would be lucky enough to gain her attention." He knew his father wouldn't like his response, but he couldn't let Bill's words about Zoe stand without defense.

Bill exhaled loudly. "Just take care of this. And do it without making Blackwell the next front-page feature or having our name plastered across every television station in the nation as breaking news. Good day, son." He snapped his suit jacket straight and stormed out of the conference room.

Ethan wanted to move but couldn't. He sat there with his mind ablaze with hot thoughts.

He was angry at how his father had put Zoe down. How he spoke of her not being on Ethan's level. He was angry at himself for losing control and letting things get this far. He was upset that he'd have to end things with Zoe.

How much of their conversation had she heard? Ethan knew she was upset. He'd seen it in her posture, in the cool way she'd entered and exited the room, in the stand-offish way she'd told them to enjoy their day without looking at them.

What would their very next conversation be like? The fun was officially over, but could he really just let her go—now?

Nineteen

When Zoe saw Ethan's number light up her cell phone again, she hesitated. He had been calling all afternoon and evening and she'd refused to answer. She'd figured a good night's sleep would help her find the words and strength to deal with what was coming but she woke in the morning feeling just as bad.

With a coffee cup in one hand and her cell phone in the other, she paced circles around her small kitchen. Finally, she paused and groaned. This was really happening. Why had she allowed it to go so far? Why had she fallen for him? She cursed the day she'd gone back to his apartment during the big storm. But she hadn't had a choice. Or had she?

Zoe grunted and put the phone down. She needed more time before she could speak to Ethan. He wasn't due to come to the office today so that would give her more time. Delaying the inevitable, she put her phone on vibrate. They had agreed that they would enjoy each other's company as long as it was possible. It had been easy to say and even easier to do. The hard part was now here—ending it all.

She had dated casually before, and when the novelty wore off, she and her former prospects had gone their own ways with no hard feelings. This was different. It felt different. Ethan was different.

Zoe knew it was time to walk away. She wondered if she actually could. She knew she didn't want to. What would it be like to work for Ethan now? And Bill. She'd heard what he'd said about her. She wasn't on their level. She already knew that. His family would never accept her. But Bill's words angered her. Who did he think he was?

Zoe plopped down in a kitchen chair and held her head in both hands. Where had she and Ethan gone wrong? They'd been careful. Had they become too familiar with one another in front of people? This had been a bad idea from the start and now her heart was stirred into the mix. She hadn't spoken to Ethan yet, so nothing was official, but she already felt her heart breaking.

Sleep had evaded her the night before. Tossing and turning, she'd finally just gotten out of bed and showered. She still had at least two hours before she needed to be at work and her drive was no more than fifteen minutes.

With the extra time, despite the lack of any real appetite, she decided to fix some breakfast. Taking eggs, butter and bread from the refrigerator, she placed everything on the counter and pulled out a small frying pan. One egg and a slice of toast would do. She just needed something in her stomach. She heated the frying pan and added a pat of butter. She pulled out a slice of multigrain toast and placed it in the toaster. When she cracked the egg on the hot skillet, the scent of it rose to her nostrils and her stomach lurched.

"Ew! That egg must be bad," Zoe said to the empty room. She tossed it in the trash, cleaned the pan out and added more butter. She cracked a second egg into the pan, but immediately the scent made her gag. A wave of nausea came over her. She instinctively covered her mouth. "Ugh! That whole carton must be bad."

Zoe tossed the entire carton. Fortunately she had a new, fresh dozen. Again, she cleaned the frying pan and cracked another egg. Again, the scent assaulted her. She wretched, covered her mouth and ran to the bathroom just in time to vomit without making a complete mess.

Zoe cleaned herself up, brushed her teeth and went back to the kitchen. She tossed the second carton of eggs out and tried to remember how long ago she'd purchased them. That last carton wasn't a week old, there was no reason the eggs should have gone bad in that short amount of time. Suddenly she wished she hadn't thrown them all out; she could have taken them back to the supermarket.

She put away the butter and pulled out milk and cereal and grabbed a bowl from the cabinet. Out of habit, Zoe opened the carton of milk and sniffed. Immediately the scent turned her stomach. This time she couldn't make it to the bathroom. She threw up in the kitchen sink.

"What the hell!" She wiped her mouth with the back of her hand.

Zoe washed her hands and headed back to the bathroom to brush her teeth again. She glanced in the mirror and the possibility hit her. Slowly, she lowered the toothbrush.

" Could I be pregnant?" she wondered in disbelief. "I can't. Get." Her mouth fell open. She stood unmoving for several moments. "Pregnant," she finally finished.

Zoe knew it was supposed to be impossible. That's what her doctor had told her and her mother when she was just a freshman in college and suffered severe pelvic pains. She'd missed half a semester of school after having to get emergency surgery. Her condition had been described as some kind of common polycystic issue. The final blow had been delivered when the doctor had said that she would probably never be able to have children. Though she hadn't been ready to be a mother then, she'd cried for days over the inability to bear future children.

Zoe stood staring in the mirror, turning the question over and over in her mind. Could she be pregnant?

She finished up in the bathroom and emailed both Ethan and her office manager to let them know she would be late. She put this one on her sick mother. No one would question that. At first she thought of going to the local pharmacy to get a test, but thought better of that. She needed to know for sure. Zoe waited until her doctor's office opened and called to ask if she could come right away.

By ten that morning, Zoe heard words she never thought she'd ever hear in her entire life. "Ms. Baldwin. Congratulations. You're pregnant!"

Congratulations! The word rang in her ears. She couldn't find a response.

The smile fell from the doctor's face. "There are options, Ms. B—"

"No. Um. Thank you. I won't be needing those options."

"Okay." The doctor sounded uncertain.

"I'm sorry. Dr. Brown. This is just a little unexpected, that's all. You know with my condition and all."

"Yes, I understand. But you know that the man upstairs always gets the final say."

Zoe offered up a weak smile. "Yes. He does." She cleared her throat before asking, "Um, how far am I?"

"Nine weeks. We're going to need to monitor this pregnancy very closely. We already know the potential for it being high risk. As you get further along, we'll see if you need to be placed on bed rest. Let's get you in for an appointment within the next week or so. Okay?" Dr. Brown's voice soothed her.

"Sure," Zoe said.

Dr. Brown patted her on her shoulder. "You'll be fine, Ms. Baldwin." She typed something in her tablet. "I'm sending over some prenatal vitamins to your pharmacy. Start taking them right away."

"Thanks, Doctor. I will."

"See you soon."

Zoe left Dr. Brown's office moving like a zombie. This was never supposed to happen. Yes, Ethan and she had gotten comfortable, or should she just call it careless. It only happened a time…or two. Most of the time they used protection. They'd never established themselves as being in a committed relationship. That was never the intention. But they knew they were only seeing each other.

Pregnant. The word played over and over in her mind.

A barrage of emotions fought to overshadow others. She felt confused, angry, hurt, overwhelmed and, of all things, excited. Excited because she was going to actually have a baby. A baby that she had been told would never be possible. And because it was likely that it might never happen again, she had no choice. She had to have Ethan's baby.

Twenty

"Ethan! What are you doing here?" Zoe scanned the block and then stepped back to let him inside her town house.

"You won't answer my calls or texts." Ethan brushed past her. He looked around her house as if he'd find clues to the questions that had been flooding his mind for the past three days. "Are you okay? Is your family all right?"

"I emailed you."

"About work." He breathed in slowly and let it out. "I've been trying to reach you for days. What's really going on, Zoe? I know you heard what my father said."

"My family is fine." Zoe turned around and headed to her kitchen. Ethan followed. "Thanks for asking."

"This is about my father, isn't it? I know. I'm sorry about that. He was wrong."

Zoe reached the counter and turned around. She

shrugged. "We said we'd stay on this ride until it was no longer fun, right? Well, the ride is over, Ethan."

"That's it?" Ethan asked, feeling himself becoming agitated. He didn't like her nonchalance. "Just like that?"

"Just like that." She threw her hands up and let them fall against her sides. "What are we supposed to do? Ugh. We knew this would happen eventually."

He huffed, closed his eyes and took a moment to calm himself. "Is this what you really want?"

She looked away. "I don't have a choice, do I?" She held her hands up in surrender.

"Listen." Ethan massaged his temples. "I apologize for my father. He shouldn't have said those things. He's just worried about our company being dragged through the mud on possible harassment charges. He's disappointed in me, not you."

"Which is why we have no choice but to end this."

"I don't want this to end!" There. He'd said it.

Zoe sat down, lifted her head toward the ceiling and groaned. "Ethan," she said quietly. "We don't have a choice. I'd never do anything to jeopardize Blackwell. It's been the best work experience of my career. I love the team. I love the work. But..."

Ethan went to her. "But what?"

"This is not good." She looked up at him and shook her head. "I want to be respected by my colleagues for what I bring to the table. Not because I'm the boss's girlfriend. I want the respect of my boss and my boss's boss. Look how weird things have been since the meeting. If he knows about us, then who else knows? It will only be a matter of time before everyone knows. I don't want to be the subject of the juicy office gossip. I don't want to be the one everyone's talking about behind my back. I've worked so hard to prove myself in this industry. I can't believe I put all of that at risk."

"We'll be more careful and I'll deal with my father," Ethan promised. "Eventually he'll come around. I know what I want. Even he can't stand in the way of that."

"It's not the same. Your father was right." She lifted one shoulder in a half shrug. "We're two different people from two different worlds. It will be no big deal for you, but for me, this will always be associated with scandal. We knew what we were getting into. Now we have to deal with the consequences. We knew this day would come. Let's just cut our losses. Give me some time and I'll find another position."

"What? Now you want to quit?" Ethan took to pacing.

"Ethan!"

"No. Don't you think that's a bit much?"

"Ugh! You don't get it, do you?"

He stopped pacing abruptly. "Then tell me what I'm missing. So people found out that we were seeing each other. We're two consenting adults." His arms flailed.

"It was an affair. There's a difference."

"An affair?" he yelled. "Neither of us are married. There was no cheating involved."

"Then why were we hiding it? It was an office affair and no matter how you look at this, others will view it with a measure of scandal. I was screwing my boss!"

"Who cares what people think?"

Zoe shot to her feet. "I do! My last name isn't Blackwell. I won't get any pardons. My career path isn't guaranteed. My parents don't own the business. My career is on the line here," she said in a lower tone. "My reputation. My job. How I'm viewed by the executive officers will be shaped by this." She sat back down. "I can't believe I let this happen."

Ethan lowered to his knees so he could be face-to-face with her. "I understand. I'm sorry. But we shouldn't stop seeing each other because of what people might think. I care about what *we* think—about each other. I realize I have an advantage. I get that. But I still want to be with you."

Zoe shook her head. "I'm sorry, Ethan. There's more at stake here than you even know."

Ethan closed his eyes and inhaled.

Zoe's cell phone rang. He lifted himself from his knees and began pacing again while she went over to the counter where she'd left the phone.

"It's my mother. I have to take this." She answered, "Hey, Ma."

Ethan heard her gasp and paused to look at her.

"Oh, my God! Call 911, I'll meet you at the hospital. I'm on my way," Zoe said frantically. "Sorry, Ethan. I have to go." Worry covered her face, and she scurried to the front of the house.

Ethan wanted to ask what happened, but it wasn't his place. He wanted to offer his help but knew she'd refuse it. "Everything okay? Is there anything I can help you with?" he asked anyway, following her.

"No. But thanks." Zoe grabbed her keys, opened the door and turned to him. "Ethan…" She stared into his eyes for a few beats. "I do care. But I can't do this. At least not this way. I'm sorry." She kissed his lips, closed her eyes. The kiss was soft. Slow. Final. She rested her cheek against his for just a moment. It felt like goodbye.

Ethan stepped out the front door and behind him Zoe locked up, then ran past him, got into her car and sped off. He watched her race down to the stop sign at the corner, pause for a brief moment and take off.

He was at a loss.

He was spoiled. Used to getting what he wanted. And he wanted Zoe.

He'd find a way to deal with his father. He hated to disappoint Bill. For all that man had done for him, he deserved Ethan's best. Torn, he fought between being faithful to his father and being faithful to his own heart.

But what difference did it make now, especially if Zoe wasn't willing to risk being with him?

Twenty-One

Shena had had a seizure. The doctor said it was a side effect of the new medication that had been prescribed for her bipolar disorder. Zoe felt terrible for pushing her to try the new meds. She only wanted her sister to feel better. Now, after a frantic night in the emergency room, Shena was finally resting peacefully in the hospital bed with her mother and Zoe at her side.

Zoe hadn't been back home since she'd run out on Ethan the night before. She tiptoed from the hospital room and headed to the family lounge so she could text him. Exhausted, she flopped into one of the chairs and pulled out her phone.

Sorry I had to run out so quickly. It was a family emergency. All is well now, but I'll need another day off to handle a few things.

She hoped that would be enough. Next she texted the office manager, Bella, and told her about the family emergency. The only thing her coworkers knew was that Zoe had a sickly mother. Her true family dynamics weren't any of their business.

Her phone buzzed. She'd received a reply from Ethan.

Sorry to hear that. Glad all is well now. Take the time you need. Anything I can do to help?

Thanks and thanks for the offer. We will be fine.

OK. I'm here if you need me.

Zoe wasn't used to the cordial tone they were using in this exchange. Their familiar, playful nature filled with sexual innuendo was gone. It hurt. Bad.

But she knew she was making the right choice. She'd find a new job and raise her baby on her own. Neither she nor Ethan had signed up for that kind of commitment and she wasn't going to stand by and let his family speak ill of her or her child.

Zoe was no longer a nervous college student. She wasn't going to sit by and allow herself to be scorned by Ethan's parents for not growing up wealthy. She already knew how Bill felt about her. It would be one thing if it was just Ethan's father, but Bill was also her boss's boss. Work would become unbearable. If they found out about the pregnancy, their opinion of her would only get worse. She wouldn't subject herself to the Blackwells' judgment of her.

She'd never imagined being a single mom—or a mom at all. Her own mother had struggled all her life raising Zoe and Shena. With Zoe's finance career, she'd manage much better than her mother had been able to on a modest blue-collar salary.

And Zoe would cherish this baby like the miracle that he or she was. Of course, she would have preferred to raise a child under better circumstances.

A new job. Zoe hated to have to look for one. She loved working for Blackwell Wealth Management. Not to mention, she made more money working for them than she had her entire career. Hopefully she'd find a job with a great boss like Ethan and nothing like Seth.

Thinking about jobs made her go to LinkedIn. She checked her profile and noted changes she needed to make. She noticed that Robert Richford had just posted and remembered meeting him at the conference a few months back. She'd connected with him on the social media platform immediately afterward, of course, and with a few others from the conference, as well. His company, Richford Financial, did similar work to Blackwell, with a few different options as to what they offered their clients.

Zoe went to his profile and wrote him a quick message about seeking opportunities with his firm. To her surprise, he responded right away.

Hi, Zoe, of course I remember you. I'd be happy to speak with you about opportunities here at Richford. Can you come by the office? Or perhaps we can meet for coffee or lunch sometime this week.

Zoe couldn't believe her luck. If she could land a job at Richford Financial, she wouldn't have to worry about hiding her pregnancy until something else came along. The sooner she could leave Blackwell, the better. She checked her work calendar on her phone.

Great. This week works. I have the most flexibility today.
Otherwise Wednesday or Thursday would work.

Zoe hit Send and waited for his response. It didn't
come as fast as the previous one. She put her phone
down, got up and walked over to the window.

The family lounge looked out over the ambulance
bay. Flashing lights colored the area. Zoe hugged herself against the coolness of the room and watched an
emergency vehicle back up to the entrance. She couldn't
see much else since the building blocked the rest of her
view. Instead, she stared at the bright lights.

She placed a hand on her stomach. A baby. She was
going to have a baby. Her mother would be the first
person she'd tell when the time was right. She already
knew this pregnancy would be risky, but she was willing to do whatever was necessary to ensure that her
baby came out just fine.

Zoe's phone buzzed. She'd gotten a message back
from Robert.

I could make today work as long as it's after 1 p.m.

She smiled.

2 pm is perfect. I can come to your office. See you then!

This was exactly what she needed.

Zoe went back to her sister's room. Her mother was
stretching in the chair she'd slept in.

"Hey, Ma. I need to head home and get myself together for work. I have a meeting I have to get to this
afternoon."

"Go ahead, honey. I'll call you if anything changes."

"Okay. I'll be back after my meeting." Zoe kissed her sister and her mother's forehead and headed home.

After making a few updates to her LinkedIn profile, she made similar changes to her résumé, and then called Willena to tell her about the opportunity.

"You want to leave Blackwell so soon?" Willena asked.

Zoe didn't want to go into the whole story but told Willena she'd explain more later. "I just wanted to get some insight about Richford before I meet with Robert. I didn't expect to be able to meet with him so quickly."

"It's a great company, but Blackwell is a better fit," Willena pointed out. "The company is expanding, and the opportunities there are endless. I think you should stay put, but it sounds like your mind is made up. Did something happen?"

Zoe closed her eyes and sighed. She decided to tell Willena the whole story. Willena had never judged her.

"Mmm-hmm," she said occasionally as Zoe spoke. "I see," she finally said. "A woman must do what a woman must do. Let me know how the interview goes. I'll call and put in a good word."

"Thank you so much, Willena. I'll call you as soon as I'm done."

Zoe ended the call and busied herself polishing her credentials until it was time to leave for her meeting with Richford Financial. She printed copies of her résumé and placed them in her bag.

The interior of Richford Financial was just as posh as Blackwell Wealth Management. Plaques of Robert featured in major finance magazines hung along the lobby walls.

Moments after Zoe arrived, she was called into his office.

"Good afternoon, Mr. Richford." Zoe reached her hand toward him.

"Good afternoon." Robert shook her hand. "Please, have a seat."

She discreetly scanned the space. Robert's office was the size of her living room at home.

"Good seeing you again," he said. "How are things over at Blackwell?"

"Actually not bad at all. There are a few changes coming down the pike and I thought it best to explore my options," she said casually. "I really want to plant my feet at a place where I can see myself staying and growing for a long time. I saw your recent post on LinkedIn and thought I should look into your firm. You've fared well in the market." Zoe didn't want to paint a bad picture of Blackwell but she couldn't say she was leaving because her secret affair with her boss had been exposed.

"Yes, we have," Robert agreed. "I see you've done your homework. So, tell me about yourself."

Zoe shared her work history, then Robert shared a bit about his career path, and the meeting turned more conversational. By the time their meeting was wrapping up, she felt like she'd been chatting with an old mentor.

"I like the way you think," Robert said at last. "I believe you'd be a great addition to the Richford team if you're willing."

"Oh, I'm definitely willing." Zoe couldn't believe her luck. It normally took weeks of multiple interviews to land a job in her field.

"When can you start?"

"I believe it would be fair to give my job proper notice. Two weeks would do."

"Great."

In her excitement, Zoe almost forgot to mention the most important thing. "Oh. Mr. Richford. There's something I should tell you."

"What is it?" His brows creased with concern.

"Um. I'm expecting. You can't tell now, but I'm due this summer. I understand if you don't—"

Robert waved off her concern. "Fine. Your benefits will be in place way before then. Congratulations!"

"Oh. Thank you, Mr. Richford. I'm looking forward to getting started." Zoe was surprised that Robert expressed no resistance to her news.

"So am I," he said with a smile.

She closed out her meeting with him and headed back to the hospital. On the way, she called Willena to let her know how the interview went.

When Zoe got back to Shena's room, her sister was awake but groggy. Zoe sent her mother home to get some rest and stayed with Shena a few more hours. Things were moving forward. Not going the way she would have liked but going the way they had to.

Now she had to find a way to tell Ethan she would be leaving. Zoe felt her heart break all over again. She was doing the right thing. Right?

Twenty-Two

Ethan tried to cleanse himself of his desire for Zoe, but it wasn't working. Her absence left gaping holes in his existence.

He was used to talking and texting with her numerous times throughout the day. They had been talking in the mornings on their way to work, continuing their banter through texts and chatting again on their way home. In the evenings, they would take turns making dinner at one another's house. Half the time, they would wake up together early the next morning and go home before heading into the office. They'd shared countless hours talking, laughing, playing cards and swapping business ideas.

Ethan had even used a few of her ideas to boost business. That was why their region was leading the company in client growth and market share. But all that had come to an abrupt end after the last management meeting.

His solution for filling her absence in his life was to work harder. However, longer hours weren't helping to fill the void. It didn't stop thoughts of Zoe from invading his mind and stealing his focus. He wanted her back.

His father had checked in with him several times about how he was "handling" the situation. Ethan was able to honestly say that he and Zoe were no longer seeing each other, but those words nearly choked him.

She avoided him at all costs. It helped some because seeing her and not being able to take her into his arms pained him. He spent as little time as possible at her office.

But today, he wouldn't be able to avoid visiting. Their branch was scheduled to meet to go over the latest numbers and prepare for another information session. Ethan had always prided himself on not allowing his emotions to interfere with business—until now.

He pulled into his designated spot in the parking lot and shut the car off. Instead of getting out, he sat back and took a deep breath, bracing himself for his encounter with Zoe.

It had been a few days since he'd last seen her. His visit to her home that evening hadn't gone well. And it had ended with her having to run out for a family emergency so he never got to finish their discussion. Since then, they'd spoken only about business. Zoe had made it clear that she wasn't interested in speaking about much more. Ethan understood her position; she didn't want to be the subject of watercooler talk.

He didn't care about people talking. He wanted to make her smile and laugh again. He craved her body and the way she made him feel in and out of bed. He longed to engage in one of their stimulating conversations over politics or the world of finance.

Ethan hadn't totally given up on them, but he felt he needed to give Zoe some space. He could only imagine how his father's words must have made her feel. But he wasn't convinced that all the things they'd shared in the past few months meant nothing to her. Walking away wasn't easy for him and he didn't believe it was any easier for her.

Finally removing the key from the ignition, Ethan pushed the car door open and headed toward the building. Inside the office, he greeted the staff as normal and headed straight for his office.

Zoe's door was closed when he passed by, and he didn't bother knocking like he normally would have. He continued to his office and shut the door behind him.

He opened his laptop, hit the power button and grabbed the television remote, pointing it to the flat screen on his wall. For the next few minutes, he took in some market updates before opening up a few documents that he would need for this meeting. The stock market had been experiencing a rough couple of days, and he knew each branch was fielding calls from clients with concerns about their investments. He added that to his agenda for the meeting. Going to his emails, his eyes scanned the words, but his brain failed to absorb any of what he read. Zoe had slipped into his thoughts again, stealing his ability to focus.

Ethan stood and walked to the window. Stuffing his hands in his pockets, he zeroed in on the intricate landscaping below. He anticipated and dreaded seeing Zoe. He looked at his watch. The meeting would start in less than fifteen minutes. He was going to need coffee.

He opened his door to head to the kitchen, and ran

right into Zoe. Their bodies collided, causing the steaming coffee in her Blackwell mug to spill all over his blue shirt.

"Whoa!" Ethan jumped back, pulling his soaked shirt away from his chest. A few staff members sitting at their cubicles jumped to their feet.

Zoe's eyes widened. "I'm so sorry." She wiped at his soiled shirt. "I was coming to tell you that Carter was trying to reach you, but you weren't answering. He asked me to see if you were in the office. Is it hot? I'm so sorry. I have wipes in my office."

Ethan felt the burn of the hot coffee, but he was more aware of the concerned look in Zoe's eyes.

"I'm fine." He looked down at his shirt and then back at Zoe and the few faces that were still directed toward him. "Believe me, I'm fine." There was a large mocha-colored stain right in the center of his shirt.

"Come. I have wipes." Zoe turned toward her office.

Ethan followed her. She retrieved some wipes stashed in her desk and, pulling a few from the package, she started toward him. He closed her office door. She paused and stared at him.

"We have to talk," he said.

"Not now, Ethan."

"Then when? You've been avoiding me. I've tried to give you space but we have to clear the air. We can't continue working like this."

Still holding the wipes, Zoe remained still. She closed her eyes and took several breaths. "Please, Ethan. Now is not a good time."

"Later. I can stop by. We need to settle this."

"Fine. Stop by later. You left a few things at the house anyway. You can pick those up."

That stung. He didn't want to remove his things from

her house. It was nothing significant but removing anything that remained would be too final.

Ethan took slow steps toward her. He stopped, leaving only a few inches between them. He wanted to kiss
her. To taste her sweet lips again. He wanted to pull her
into his arms. What had she done to him? Why couldn't
he just walk away?

They were close enough for him to feel her breath.
Zoe didn't move. She seemed cemented in place. He
watched her swallow. Watched her neck shift. She
tucked her bottom lip into her mouth and gnawed.

Ethan took the wipes from her hands. They remained
close. Inches apart. Being near her was electrifying. He
wanted to touch her cheek, caress her face. He affected
her; he could tell by the way her chest rose and fell now
that he was so close. Her breathing changed, and she
avoided his eyes.

He was glad there was still some impact. For him,
that meant it wasn't over. All hope wasn't lost. He fought
the urge to kiss her. He missed the feeling of her in his
arms.

Zoe still hadn't spoken. She just stood there, breathing with more urgency.

"Tonight," Ethan said.

Zoe cleared her throat. "Tonight."

"Thank you." He leaned forward, compelled by a
force, by his desire to be with her. His wet shirt sticking to him no longer mattered.

She didn't move, showed no sign of resistance.

Gently he placed his lips on hers. She didn't pull
away, and Ethan kissed her. A soft peck. When he pulled
back, her eyes were closed. "Tonight," he repeated.

Leaving with the wipes, he rubbed at the stains in his shirt on the way out. She hadn't resisted him. Tonight, perhaps they could make things right.

Twenty-Three

Zoe checked her phone and ignored yet another text from Ethan. She had dodged him the night before. She just couldn't have handled seeing him after he'd kissed her in the office earlier that day. The kiss had made it hard for her to concentrate in her meetings. It had also entangled her thoughts into a jumbled mess. Zoe knew that she needed to face him sooner or later, but she had to buy some time. She'd meant to give him her letter of resignation, but couldn't bring herself to do that just yet either. None of this was easy.

She'd planned on making a clean break. Avoiding him was part of the process. But his kiss. That soft, sweet kiss had reminded her of how much she missed him. And now that she was sitting in the doctor's office with his baby growing inside of her, she definitely couldn't deal with him. She'd answer his texts when she got home.

Zoe looked at the couple sitting in the waiting room across from her. The woman took her husband's hand and placed it on her belly. "Feel that?" she asked.

The husband's face beamed. "Yep." He lowered his face to her stomach. "We're going to have to put you in football with a kick like that, buddy."

The two of them gushed over their baby. When he sat back, she rested her head on his shoulder, and they held hands.

The scene was sweet and intimate. Witnessing it made Zoe feel like an intruder. It also made her sad. Her story would never look like theirs. She was going to be a single mom.

She'd thought about not telling Ethan about the baby at all but figured she wouldn't be able to get away with that for too long. Unless she moved, she couldn't hide a baby forever. She'd tell him when the time was right, but she wouldn't dare expect anything from him. She'd show him and his family that she and her baby could manage without them. Bill wouldn't have to worry about her not being on their level. Based on the compensation outlined in the offer letter she'd received from Richford Financial, she could take care of her baby just fine by herself.

Another couple came in holding hands. Their excitement was written across their faces. This gentleman helped his very pregnant wife to her seat and supported her back as she sat carefully. He looked down and saw that her shoelace was untied. Without hesitation, he got on one knee and tied her shoe. Seeming grateful, she smiled, and he placed his arm around her neck when he sat next to her.

Zoe hadn't expected to feel so alone on this appointment. She wished things were different. Ethan could have been right there with her.

Truth be told, Zoe was scared. She'd heard all kinds of stories about being pregnant and she already knew her pregnancy wasn't going to be easy. Scar tissue from her surgery years ago posed a threat. Dr. Brown had used expressions like *monitor closely*, *high risk* and *possible bed rest*. She had no idea what all of that really entailed. She just knew this could be her only chance at bearing a child, so she had to take it.

Her need to have this baby didn't have to impact Ethan's life, so whenever she told him, she'd also let him know she didn't need him. He claimed he wanted to be with her, but would he still feel the same way when he found out she was pregnant?

Getting his employee pregnant during a secret affair certainly wouldn't fit into his family's perfect little setup. And Zoe could only imagine what his father would have to say about it. This was why she needed to leave Blackwell ASAP. It wasn't because she really wanted to go.

A nurse called Zoe's name, snatching her from her thoughts. She took one last look at the happy-looking couples before following the nurse into an examination room. The woman took her vitals and then gave her a paper gown and told her to undress. She assured her that the doctor would be with her soon and closed the door. Zoe flinched when the door shut. The small room seemed to close in on her.

Dr. Brown arrived a few minutes later. "Hey there, Ms. Baldwin. How are we doing this week?"

"All right. A little tired. I didn't get good sleep last night."

"We need to work on that. Baby is going to need you to get your rest."

The doctor examined her, and Zoe paid close attention in wide-eyed awe. This was all so new to her. She didn't really know what to expect.

"So far everything seems fine, Ms. Baldwin, but we're not going to take any chances. I'd like to see you every two to three weeks as opposed to monthly. When you hit your third trimester, I want to see you every week. Okay? Any questions for me?"

"Yes. Plenty. I don't even know where to start." Zoe released a nervous laugh.

"Start with the one that scares you most."

"Okay…" She unloaded all of her questions on Dr. Brown, who patiently listened and thoroughly answered, making her feel a little better. "And those vitamins you gave me," Zoe added, "they make me nauseous."

"Okay. I'll give you a new prescription. Make sure you're taking them after you've eaten. They don't do well on empty stomachs. I'll send it right over to your pharmacy. Anything else?"

"I think that's all for now."

"Well, congratulations again. To say this pregnancy is unexpected is an understatement. I imagine you two must be ecstatic. I can't wait until this little miracle bundle arrives."

Zoe forced a smile. "Yes. Me, too. Thanks."

Dr. Brown's comment brought Ethan to mind. Zoe doubted he'd be ecstatic.

She went straight to the pharmacy before going home. Back in the car, she opened her new prescription and took a look at the pills. They were huge. Zoe grunted. She hated taking pills, especially large ones. She tossed the bottle in her bag and started her car. Her phone chimed again. It was another text from Ethan. She'd read them at home.

She stepped inside her town house, placed her purse

on the couch and went to the kitchen for crackers and water. She came back, plopped on the couch and turned on the television. She munched on a few crackers before popping one of her enormous vitamins and washing that and the crackers down with water.

This was one of the few nights that she hadn't planned to go by her mother's house. Shena had begun to do much better after her recent hospital stint, giving Zoe and her mother less to worry about.

Zoe realized she had dozed off when she heard the doorbell ring. Lack of sleep from the night before had caught up to her. She got up to answer the door, peeked out and saw that it was Ethan.

She braced herself a moment before opening the door. She'd avoided him last night. Tonight, she'd have to face him.

"Hello," Ethan greeted her cautiously.

"Hi, Ethan." Zoe stepped back.

"I texted you…a few times," he said, still standing in the entrance.

"I know."

"Can I come in?"

"Sure." Zoe turned and went back to the living room and sat on the couch. She muted the sound. "I'm sorry about your shirt."

"It was nothing my cleaners couldn't handle." Silence settled between them for a moment. "I'm sorry, too."

She shrugged. She knew Ethan was referring to the kiss. She couldn't really say she was sorry about that. She just couldn't let it happen again or she'd have to re-align her thoughts once more.

"Can I sit?"

It wasn't until then that she noticed he was still standing. She shifted closer to the end of the couch, pushing up against her purse to could make room for him.

"We need to work this out," he said.

"I thought we did that."

"No. We didn't. You had an emergency and we never finished our conversation. How's your mother by the way?"

"She's fine. Thanks for asking." Zoe looked away from him.

Ethan held his hand up. "I know you were angry. I wanted to give you, and quite honestly me, as well, some time to think. We work together. You're a huge asset to the company. We need to be able to work together *and* I don't want to lose you. We can take this as slowly as you need to. Don't worry about my father. This is about you and me."

"Ethan." Zoe pressed her lips together. This was harder than she'd anticipated. "I took another job."

"You what?" He reared back. Hurt registered across his face. "Why?"

"Because. I needed to. I wanted to tell you before now. I'll email my official letter of resignation to you tomorrow. We don't have to worry about your father. Now we can both just move on."

Ethan opened his mouth, but no words came out. He blinked, looked around the room, then directed his gaze back at Zoe. He looked genuinely confused. "Why?"

"It was the best thing."

He blew out a sharp exhale. "Where?"

"Richford Financial."

Ethan's face morphed through several emotions right before Zoe's eyes. "Richford. Are you kidding me?"

"Yes. What's wrong with Richford?"

"Please. Whatever you do, don't go to Richford. Let's just work this out."

"I've already accepted the offer."

"This isn't happening." Ethan stood and paced with both hands on his hips. After a few laps, he sat back down and took both Zoe's hands into his.

His touch sent Zoe's emotions reeling once again. "Ethan, please don't do this."

"This is about more than Richford. If you're going to leave Blackwell, that's the last place I want you to go. But here's what I need to say." Ethan took a breath. "I don't want us to be a secret. You're not a fling to me or some scandalous office affair. I want to be with you. Tell me you don't have feelings for me."

Zoe dropped her head. She couldn't say she felt nothing. That lie wouldn't pass her lips. She lifted her head. Instead, she said, "I can't. I just can't do this. I'm sorry."

He looked to the ceiling and back at her. He still had her hands in his. Zoe fought back tears. She had to stand her ground.

"Okay." His voice was solemn. "Fine." He stood.

Zoe couldn't look at his face. His pain threatened to make her go back on what she'd decided. She stood also, knocking over her bag. She hated this. She felt awful.

Ethan's face changed as he stared at her bag. That painful looked changed into one of curiosity. He tilted his head. "What's that?" he asked, pointing near her feet.

Zoe looked down and noticed the contents of her purse had spilled beside it. The bottle of vitamins had rolled and stopped right at her foot. It was too late to mask the large Prenatal label on the bottle.

"Zoe, are you pregnant?"

Her mouth opened but instead of speaking, she clamped it shut.

"Zoe!" Ethan stepped closer to her. "Are. You. Pregnant?"

In a small voice, she answered, "Yes."

Ethan stepped back as if someone had pushed him. His breath became ragged. All the air seemed to have left the room at once. Zoe could hardly breathe herself.

"Don't worry, Ethan," she said in a rush. "I won't ask you for anything. Your father, your family won't have to be bothered with me or my child. We will be just fine."

"Your child?" His voice boomed. Zoe flinched. His voice lowered. "It's my child, too, isn't it?"

Zoe didn't answer right away.

"Isn't it?" he asked again.

"Yes." She instinctively hugged herself.

Ethan sat slowly—very slowly. "You were going to run off and have this baby by yourself? You weren't going to tell me?"

"Your family. I—"

"This has nothing to do with my family." He stood again and started pacing. "This is about us. Our relationship—and now our baby. And you thought it made sense to keep this from me? You're carrying my baby." He looked confused. Then he smiled. "I'm going to have a baby."

Zoe was confused by his reaction.

"How long have you known about this?"

Zoe groaned. "A few days."

Ethan shook his head. "Why?"

"Because we're not on the same level, okay?" Zoe couldn't help the tears. "I won't have my child being treated like an outcast because his own grandfather doesn't think his mother is good enough. We may not have as much as your family but my baby deserves to be loved and accepted. I don't come from a perfect family but that doesn't make us less than anyone." She

stabbed the air with her index finger. "I won't have it."
She couldn't catch her breath. "I know what rejection
feels like and I'd rather raise my child alone than allow
him to be treated like he's less than!" She felt the fresh
sting of her father's abandonment.

"Zoe! Zoe! Zoe!"

He'd called her name three times before Zoe realized it. He wrapped his arms around her, and she cried
into his chest.

"I would never let that happen to you or our baby either," he said. "I'd never let anyone mistreat our child.
You think my family is perfect? We're not. Let me be
the father our baby needs. Don't take that from me."

Zoe tried to speak through the tears. She wanted to
believe him.

"Zoe, I care about you," he went on. "I have feelings
for you—deep feelings for you. I can't believe that you
don't feel the same. I knew it when I kissed you yesterday." He held her at arm's length and looked into her
crying eyes. "Zoe. I love you. No one will ever hurt you
or our baby. I'll make sure of that."

Zoe knew she was being emotional…but had she just
heard him say that he loved her?

Twenty-Four

Ethan was going to be a father. That single thought had consumed him from the moment he'd left Zoe's house the night before. The news excited and frightened him. He'd imagined a family—wife, a few kids. He hadn't been expecting to start one this soon, but what better woman to start one with? He wondered if he would be a good father.

Ethan was sure Zoe would make a great mom. He could go on for days about the great qualities she possessed. His child stood to inherit many of those same great characteristics. Zoe was smart, determined, beautiful, family oriented and even a bit stubborn. And thanks to her breakdown in front of him last night, Ethan understood her even more.

What Zoe didn't realize was that Ethan was much more like her than she knew. He knew the sting of rejection and abandonment as well as she did, which was

why he was at Robert Richford's office this morning.
Ethan hadn't bothered to call. He'd just shown up, wanting to catch Robert there.

"Good morning. I'm here to see Robert Richford,"
Ethan said to the woman in the posh reception area.
Frosted glass framed in dark wood separated the area
from the rest of the office. He strived to remain composed. Normally that wasn't an issue for him, but he
had no idea how this meeting would go. The last time
he'd approached Robert, years before, it hadn't gone the
way he'd wanted it to.

"Good morning!" The woman's warm greeting and
soothing voice generated an involuntary smile. "Is Mr.
Richford expecting you?"

"No. But if you could please let him know that Ethan
Blackwell is here to see him and it's urgent, I'd appreciate it."

"Sure. Just give me one moment." The woman got up
and disappeared through frosted double doors.

Ethan second-guessed his decision to come see Robert. Perhaps he should just leave. Immediately, he tossed
that thought from his mind. He had waited long enough.
This was the best time to have this conversation. He
would leave once he got what he came for.

Moments later, the receptionist returned and invited
Ethan to follow her across the office.

"Mr. Blackwell is here to see you," she said at an open
door. She woman stepped aside, smiled and nodded at
Ethan. "Good day to you, sir." She waved her hand for
him to step into Robert's office.

"Thanks." Ethan walked inside. He looked around,
taking in the multiple flat screens displaying various
financial news channels. Robert's office looked as if
an interior designer had decorated it. It was a cross be-

tween a presidential suite and a home draped in traditional elegance.

Robert stood behind a large mahogany desk. Two burgundy tufted-leather chairs faced it on the opposite side. Robert muted the TVs with a touch of a button. Silenced reporters from various financial news stations reported the status of the stock market.

Robert rounded his desk. "Ethan." He reached out to shake hands.

Ethan paused a moment before taking Robert's hand and shaking it. Instead of going back to his chair, Robert sat on the edge of the desk. He motioned for Ethan to sit.

"You look good," Robert said.

"I didn't come for the flattery, but thanks." Ethan's tone was a bit sharp. He inhaled to remain composed.

"What brings you here this morning, son?"

"Please don't call me that."

Robert raised his hands in surrender. "Sorry."

"Zoe Baldwin," Ethan said.

"What about her? I'm looking forward to having her join the team. Seems like she'll be a real asset."

Ethan paused for a moment pondering the right way to ask his question. "What made you hire her?"

Robert's brows furrowed. "She's a great candidate. Her résumé was impressive. Why?"

"You knew she worked for Blackwell, right?"

"Of course, but what does that have to do with anything?" Robert asked.

"Did she come to you or did you solicit her?"

Robert looked as if he were becoming annoyed with Ethan's line of questioning. "I'm not out here trying to poach on Blackwell's talent pool. What's this about, son?"

Ethan flinched inwardly when Robert said the word

son. "Nothing. She's been an asset to the company. I'm sorry to see her go." Ethan hoped his response sufficed. He didn't want to appear defeated.

Robert nodded. "I see."

"I also have a few other questions," Ethan added. Robert raised a brow but didn't seem surprised. "I need to know."

Robert took a deep breath. "Now?"

"Yes. This is as good a time as any. I want to hear it from you. I was young when I came to you before and you refused to see me."

Robert lifted himself from the edge of the desk and put one hand in the pocket of his tailored slacks. "Have you spoken to your parents?"

"I deserve to hear the truth from you."

Robert walked toward a window and looked out. It took a few moments, but he finally spoke. "I was wrong. We both were. Perhaps we all were. It was a moment of weakness and horrible judgment."

Ethan waited for him to continue.

"We were friends...your mother, father and me. They started having issues and your mother had taken to coming to me to discuss them. We had been friends even longer than your father and me. I was supposed to talk some sense into your dad but instead I became emotionally attached to her. I was also going through problems with my wife at the time. With the situation at hand and wild emotions, before we knew it, your mother and I had made the biggest mistakes of our lives."

Robert paused and drew in a long breath. "My marriage ended up in divorce. Your mother and father were lucky enough to work things out. It was a long time before we even acknowledged the reality that you could be mine. I kept asking. I wanted to know."

Ethan listened intently. He'd only heard bits and pieces of this story previously. Bill refused to address it, telling Ethan that all he needed to know was that he was Bill's son and that he loved him. His mother, Lydia, admitted the affair when Ethan approached her as a teen but refused to speak more of it.

"It was years before I knew for sure," Robert went on. "Before they admitted it to me. Since Bill and Lydia reconciled, all he wanted was for me to stay away from them and you. Somehow, we all thought it was better to leave things alone. You knew Bill as your father. He was taking good care of you. I had a new family of my own. We figured no one would ever know anyway. That was until you came to me. You were a teenager then." He sat down on the desk again and paused longer this time. "I'd signed papers. You were legally Bill's child. I couldn't say anything to you. That's the only reason I sent you away that day. I dreaded that and could only imagine how you must have felt."

"My mother told me," Ethan said. "I hounded her after overhearing something my father said. That's when I started snooping around. I found you. I understood enough to know that Bill wasn't my real dad."

He felt something shift inside of him. All these years, he'd believed that Robert had just rejected him, and now he knew that wasn't the case. There was more to this story. He needed to speak to his father now.

"Thanks," Ethan said, standing. He had gotten what he'd come for. What more was there to say?

"Ethan," Robert called as he made his way to the door.

Ethan turned around.

"Why now?"

"I'm going to be a father."

Robert nodded. That seemed to be all the explanation he needed.

Ethan headed for the door again.

"Ethan," Robert called to his back. "For what it's worth, I may not have been able to show it, but I've always watched from the shadows. You'd make any father proud."

Ethan went back to his office. After work he drove to his parents' home. He'd timed his visit so that he would catch Bill just as he arrived home. He'd checked in with his mother on the way and knew she wouldn't be home. He wanted to speak with Bill alone.

Ethan pulled up behind his father just as Bill entered his three-car garage.

"Hey, son!" Bill waved as he got out of the car.

"We need to talk," Ethan said as he got out.

Bill paused. "Everything okay? Should I pour us a drink?" he said jokingly.

"Perhaps. It's about Robert Richford."

Bill lifted his brow and sighed. Slowly he closed his car door. "That."

"Yes, sir. That."

"Let's go into my office."

Ethan followed his father inside. His mother's stylish touch was all over their home. Even when she wasn't there, he could feel her presence. She was out tonight, as she often was, schmoozing on behalf of several non-profit organizations where she served as a member of the board.

Bill filled two rocks glasses halfway with scotch. He handed one to Ethan and sat on a love seat.

"Can we get right to it?" Ethan wanted to save the small talk for another time.

"I forgave your mother," Bill said at once. "I loved her. Still love her with everything in me. We worked things out in our marriage and vowed to stick together from that point forward. Sticking with my wife, meant sticking with you—*our* son," Bill emphasized.

Ethan sipped his scotch. He looked at Bill, waiting for him to continue.

"I was building the business and wasn't around often at all. I imagine your mother got quite lonely. We had our issues," Bill admitted. "In the end, we didn't want to complicate things so we agreed that Robert would be completely removed from the picture."

"To save face."

Bill tilted his head. "You can say that." He leaned forward. "Ethan, you *are* my son. I never wanted you to feel any different than your brothers and sister."

"Yet, I always did."

Bill dropped his head but lifted it back up. "I'm sorry."

"I guess none of us are perfect, are we?"

It took a moment, but Bill finally nodded in agreement. "What made you bring this up now?"

"It's the right time." Ethan paused and considered his words. He knew that what he was about to say would hit his father hard. "Zoe is pregnant. She's no fling to me. No careless affair. I care about her—a lot. I want you to know and respect that."

Silence expanded between them.

Ethan was glad to get that off his chest. "We can talk more later. Right now, I have to go."

"Of course." Bill sighed, sat back and took another sip of his scotch.

Ethan wasn't sure how Bill was taking the news. His response didn't offer much in the way of how he felt.

"Thanks, Dad." Ethan held his hand out to his father.

Bill took it, but instead of shaking his hand, he got up and hugged Ethan. "I love you, son."

"I love you, too, Dad."

"And I respect your decision."

Ethan felt lighter than he had in days, possibly years. He left his father and headed straight for Zoe's house. There would be no covering up the fact that she was having his baby.

There was so much he'd suspected about the situation between his parents and his biological father but hadn't had confirmed until now. Many times he had tried to convince himself that none of it mattered. But it did, especially now that he was going to be a father himself.

He'd made several attempts to speak to his mother about it over the years, but it always seemed too difficult for her. Ethan hated the sadness that consumed her when he broached the subject. That trip he'd made to Robert's home as a young man had left him broken. When Robert had refused to speak to him, Ethan had taken on the armor of rejection. Though Bill had never really treated him differently than his siblings, knowing that he wasn't his biological father had still made Ethan feel like an outsider.

Bill didn't have to accept him, but he had. So Ethan felt obligated to be as little a burden to him as possible. That was where his desire to please his dad had come from.

How could Ethan have known that was an orchestrated arrangement? He sympathized with his mother. Somehow, he'd understood even as a teen the guilt that had taken hold of her. Until today, his mother was the only person he had spoken to about this.

These questions had lingered for years. However, becoming a father made it necessary to finally seek answers and Ethan was glad that he had. Knowing helped him understand himself. He needed that going into fatherhood.

He reached Zoe's house just as the sun was setting. She opened the door and stepped aside to let him in. Lifting on her toes, she greeted him with a cordial kiss on the cheek. It wasn't the passionate greeting he'd grown accustomed to, but it was warmer than the distant space they'd settled into over the past few days.

"I have some things I need to tell you," Ethan said. He took Zoe by the hand, led her to the living room and sat her down. He was pulling back the curtain on his own truth.

Twenty-Five

Zoe couldn't believe what Ethan has just told her. She didn't even know how to respond. She guessed it was her own fault for thinking that the Blackwells were flawless just because they were wealthy. They were just like any other family. Perhaps even just like hers. She could see the pain in Ethan's eyes as he revealed family secrets that had plagued him for years. She also saw his relief in getting the information out in the open.

Zoe just listened as he spoke, not wanting to interrupt him. When he stopped, she waited several more moments to make sure he didn't have anything else to say. Then she hugged him.

She wrapped her arms around him and pulled him in tight, fighting back tears. He held her just as tight. They stayed that way, holding on to each other as if their lives depended on it. The embrace felt like therapy.

"So what now?" she said when she finally pulled away.

"If you'll have me," he began, "I say we proudly raise our baby. Stay in this together."

Ethan's words made her heart smile. But to make sure the air was truly clear of secrets, Zoe had some of her own to share.

"There are things that I should also tell you," she began.

"Tell me."

So Zoe told Ethan her truth, sharing the story of her own father walking out on her family when she and Shena were kids. The difference was, she'd never seen her father again. They'd received word that he'd died as a result of a work accident when she was in college. Unlike with Ethan, there'd been no kind of reconciliation. Zoe also shared Shena's condition with him and finally told him about how she'd thought she would never be able to have children.

"So we're having a miracle baby?"

Zoe threw her head back and laughed. "Yes." When their laughter died down, she continued, "We're a tight, loving bunch—my mom, my sister and me. We have our issues, our share of struggles. My family means the world to me. And I'm not ashamed of them."

"You shouldn't be." Ethan ran the back of his finger down her cheek.

"I guess the lesson here is that none of us are perfect," Zoe said.

"And I want to be imperfect with you." He kissed her. "And our baby. When I said I loved you the other night, I meant it."

Zoe blinked. Tears tickled her eyes. She'd realized how much she cared for Ethan in his absence. They'd spent months together, day and night. Ethan made her feel like no man had ever made her feel before. Being tough and trying to protect her heart and her child, she'd tried to fight those feelings. But when he'd said those words that night, she'd realized that she loved him, too.

"I love you, too, Ethan."

He grabbed her, wrapped his arms around her and kissed her deeply.

When he let go, Zoe touched her stomach, gazing down at it. "I still can't believe it. I'm hardly showing but I can't wait to feel my child."

"And both his parents will always be there for him."

Ethan's words touched her, but she couldn't resist. "His? Who said it will be a boy?" she teased.

"Boy, girl or frog. It doesn't matter to me. I'll be there. If it's a frog, we'll build a pond in the backyard and make sure it's got a nice pad. Get it?"

Zoe swatted Ethan playfully for the silly pun. She tried not to laugh but did anyway. "Whose backyard are we building this lush lily pad in?"

"Ours!" Ethan declared. "We're in this thing together, right?"

Zoe looked at him with a raised brow. "Don't feel obligated to stick around because you knocked me up," she teased. Ethan's mouth dropped open. "As long as you'll have me," she said with a smile.

He smiled back. "I think I'd like to keep you around for a while."

Zoe laughed again and Ethan kissed her right in the middle of it. He pulled her close.

"We have to tell our families," he said, still holding Zoe in his arms."

"Yeah," she agreed.

"And we have to do it together," he added.

"Hmm. Yeah." Her mother and sister would be ecstatic. But despite what she now knew, she wasn't looking forward to having the conversation with Ethan's parents.

They kissed again. Ethan's lips on hers felt like healing to her soul.

He pulled back long enough to say breathlessly, "I've missed you."

Immediately she felt her body respond. "Show me how much." She let seduction sparkle in her eyes. She craved what she'd missed about him.

Ethan picked her up, carried her to bed, laid her down and showed her just how much he'd missed her.

Zoe had made it to twelve weeks. She sat in Dr. Brown's waiting room with Ethan at her side, holding her hand. There was so much about the moment that filled her up. She looked at the ceiling and blinked. She insisted on containing her emotions.

"Zoe Baldwin," the nurse called.

"That's me." She and Ethan rose and followed the nurse to an examination room.

Zoe watched him take in all the equipment in the room, still holding her hand. "Babe," she said at last. "I can't put on this gown if you don't let go of my hand."

"Oh. Right." He let go of her hand.

She laughed. Ethan had exhibited this nervous energy ever since he'd picked her up for the appointment. She thought it was cute. Zoe stepped out of her clothes and into the paper gown. Dr. Brown tapped lightly on the door just as Zoe slid onto the examination table.

"Come in."

"Good morning!" Dr. Brown's cheerful tone rang through the small room. She held her hand out to Ethan.

"I'm the proud dad," he said.

Zoe rolled her eyes and chuckled. "Good morning, Dr. Brown. This is my boyfriend, Ethan Blackwell."

"Nice to meet you, proud Dad." Dr. Brown shook his hand. "Have you ever seen an ultrasound before?"

"No. Never. I don't even know what that is," Ethan admitted.

Zoe smiled at his curious nature. She loved him more than she knew was possible.

"Well, you'll learn all about it today," Dr. Brown said.

For the rest of the quick visit, Zoe watched Ethan take everything in with a sense of awe. His face lit up at the grayscale images of their baby moving around in her belly. He seemed enthralled at the thunderous sounds emanating from the sonogram. And at the end, when Dr. Brown cleaned the gel from Zoe's belly and left the room, Ethan wrapped his arms around Zoe before she could even get dressed.

"We're having a baby," he said as if the reality of it all had just sunk in.

His excitement warmed her heart. "And now we've been cleared to share the news." That thought made her anxious but happy.

He kissed her, and she giggled and melted into his embrace. She hadn't imagined ever having a man like Ethan and certainly had never imagined having his child.

Twenty-Six

Zoe was nervous. She could hardly take in the beautiful drive leading up to Ethan's parents' home. They'd passed several lavish estates and finally turned into a private driveway that was so inconspicuous she would have passed right by it if she hadn't been in the car with Ethan.

An expansive and sophisticated Colonial stretched out before them as they drove closer. The beige brick made the home look stately yet welcoming. Zoe gasped. She couldn't believe this was where they lived. By the time Ethan came to a stop, her leg was bouncing. She didn't know how the nervous energy would manifest next.

"Oh, my this is lovely," said Zoe's mother, Laura, from the back seat.

"Wow! It's huge," Shena said. She was having a good day. Zoe was happy about that.

Ethan exited the car and helped Laura and Shena out before taking Zoe's hand and leading her to the double entry doors.

The door opened before he could ring the bell.

"Hey, baby!" A short, caramel-skinned woman with salt-and-pepper hair opened the door and embraced him.

"Hey, Ma." Ethan hugged her and kissed her forehead. "This is Zoe." He presented her to his mother. "Zoe, this is my beautiful mother, Lydia."

"Let me see this gorgeous young woman." Lydia moved Ethan aside to take Zoe in. She scanned her from head to toe, then turned to Ethan with an approving nod. "You know how to pick 'em, babe!" Her laugh was more like a cackle. It was infectious, causing Zoe, Ethan, her mother and her sister to all laugh with her. Zoe liked her already.

"It's good meeting you, Mrs. Blackwell."

"Nice meeting you, honey. Come on in here." She held out her arms. Zoe stepped into her embrace.

"And you must be her mother," Lydia said after hugging Zoe. "I see where she gets her looks from."

Laura snickered. "Yes! You're looking pretty good yourself, young lady." Lydia had brought out the playful side of Laura, something Zoe hadn't seen in a while. She liked Lydia even more. "It's a pleasure to meet you, Lydia. My name is Laura. And this—" she turned around "—is my other daughter, Shena."

"The pleasure is mine." Lydia hugged Laura and Shena in turn. She ushered them all inside. Zoe gaped in awe at an elegant set of stairs winding its way up to the second floor. She had only seen homes like this in movies.

"Hey, Zoe!" Carter rounded the corner. He hugged her.

A tall gentleman who looked just like Ethan appeared just behind Carter. Zoe assumed he was their older brother, Lincoln. After him came a pretty, curvy woman with two kids at her legs. The way she lovingly clung to Lincoln gave Zoe the impression that she was probably his significant other. The huge diamond on her finger let her know that she was his wife.

Almost the entire family was gathered in the large two-story foyer, including Ethan's sister, Ivy. Lydia led the greetings, introducing everyone from both families. They all passed around hugs.

Bill was the last to enter the foyer. His brawny stature was intimidating, and his deep voice boomed when he spoke. Zoe found herself holding her breath when he approached her.

Zoe lifted her head to meet his gaze when he stood before her. She wouldn't stand down. Seconds ticked by and silence settled around them. Zoe was keenly aware that all eyes were on them.

Bill cracked first. A small smiled eased at the corners of his lips and he narrowed one eye at her. She tried to hold her smile back and narrowed an eye back at him.

"Come here, young lady." He opened his arms wide. Zoe stepped in. His bear hug felt like the warmth of a summer day and she hugged him back.

"You don't scare me, old man," she teased.

Everyone laughed, and Bill released her. "Welcome to our home. We need you back on the Blackwell team," he said right away. "We can feel the impact of your departure already."

"Dad!" Ethan scolded.

"All right, all right. No business talk today." Bill leaned down closer to Zoe's ear and pretended to whisper. "We can talk about that later. I'll pay you more than Ethan did."

Laughter filled the grand home once again.

Lydia and Ivy led them to a large room with glass doors overlooking a spacious yard. Even with the barren trees and no flowers in bloom, the yard still seemed meticulously manicured. The men went out on the deck, the winter mild enough for jackets only. Lincoln's children ran around on the grass while the ladies talked inside.

Lydia handed out mimosas. "It's Sunday, so why not call it a brunch, and what's a brunch without mimosas," she said. "Enjoy. Our meal will be ready shortly."

Laura happily accepted. Zoe and Shena politely declined. Shena had been so much better at trying to stay well. Zoe was so proud of her sister.

"I heard you made quite an impact helping to grow your territory, Zoe," Lydia said. "Kudos to you." She held her flute in the air.

"Thank you, Ms. Lydia. We had a great leader and an amazing team."

"Oh, don't be modest, honey. I understand it was all you. Take your credit. It's a poor dog that can't wag its own tail."

"Oh. Well. Okay. Yes, ma'am. And thank you." Zoe chuckled.

Lydia winked at Laura before saying to Zoe, "I also understand that you overheard my husband say some things that weren't so nice."

Zoe paused as her glass was on its way to her mouth.

"Don't worry about him," Lydia went on. "He means well. Sometimes he forgets he came from a little town in South Carolina that most people never heard of. The day we met, he called me a sassy city girl. I told him he was nothing but a country bumpkin. It was love at first sight! Ha!" Lydia's laugh was sharp and jovial.

"Our first apartment could fit in this room." Lydia

looked around. "But we made it work. We hit Wall Street with a strong sense of determination and an even stronger desire to make enough money to call our own shots. It took a little hard work, lots of struggle and even more luck. We climbed that corporate ladder together and set out to start our own business. I got out of the industry a few years ago. Finance can be grueling. I was over it." Lydia took a sip. "So don't let him fool you. He's a good man who wants the best for his children. He just needs to be reminded about where he came from every now and then."

A thin older woman entered the room. "Brunch is served."

"Thank you, Melanie," Lydia said. She walked over to the sliding doors, tapped and waved the men in. "Let's eat!"

The family gathered at a table large enough to fit all of them. Bill said grace and everyone dug into the delicious food. By the end of the meal, they had all eased into comfortable conversation.

Carter lifted his wineglass. "Let me be the first to say congratulations to Ethan for winning the competition. I have to give your team credit for building an incredible base out here on Long Island. You deserve your new position."

"Thanks," Ethan said with pride.

"Cheers!" the rest of the family chimed in.

"I'm proud of you, son," Bill added. "Congrats to the new vice president of Blackwell Wealth Management."

"Speech!" Ivy clinked her glass with a knife.

"All I have to say is," Ethan said dramatically, "Carter, where are my new irons?"

The family all laughed, knowing about the brothers' bet of a golf cart and a new set of premium clubs.

"It's on its way, bro," Carter said good-naturedly.

"No, really," Ethan said, a little more serious. "I want to say thank you to Carter for giving me a run for my money. You're a great businessman. Mom and Dad, thanks for teaching me all you know about building a business. You're the best mentors on and off the job. Zoe, thank you for bringing home the win. If it weren't for your great ideas, Carter's region might have kicked our butts! We couldn't have done it without you."

"Damn right! That position in my office is still open, Zoe," Carter joked.

"I'm good, Carter. Thanks," Zoe teased.

"I do have other announcements I'd like to make." Ethan looked at Zoe sitting by his side, and corrected himself. "That we'd like to make." He took her hand and pulled her closer.

"Dad, this will make you happy. In light of my promotion, Zoe has agreed to return to Blackwell and take on the position of vice president for the Long Island territory."

"That's my girl!" Bill raised a glass. "Welcome back. You sure are a tough negotiator and I like it!"

Zoe laughed. Lydia shook her head at her husband.

"You all may know," Ethan said, getting everyone's attention again. "Zoe and I have been seeing each other for quite some time. Well before anyone ever knew. We fell hard and fast for one another and built our relationship at the same time we built the Long Island offices. I'm happy to say that both our relationship and the company are thriving. We had some ups and downs and learned some valuable lessons in the process."

Ethan looked over at his mother and father. With smiles plastered on their faces, they nodded in agreement. "We realized that we're not perfect," he went on, "but we're perfect for each other."

Zoe rubbed his arm. "Perfectly imperfect," she said.

"Aww, how sweet," Ivy said. "Who is this guy and what did he do with my obnoxious brother?"

More laughter rang out around the table.

"It was important for us to have both our families here with us today to meet each other and hear our other special announcement," Zoe chimed in.

She zeroed in on her mother's face, ready to see her expression when they announced her pregnancy. Everyone else quieted and listened closely.

"Mom," Ethan said, nodding at her.

Lydia got up. She grinned and winked at Zoe and disappeared from the room.

Zoe was confused. They were supposed to announce the baby. What was Ethan up to?

Lydia returned with a large Tiffany box wrapped in their signature white ribbon. She placed it in front of Ethan. Zoe wondered what was in it. It clearly wasn't a ring box.

He handed the box to Zoe. She looked at it and back at him.

"Open it," he encouraged.

She opened the box and found a sterling silver rattle. She chuckled.

"We're..." Ethan started.

"...having a baby," Zoe finished with him.

Laura's eyes lit up. Lydia smiled hard, despite the fact that she obviously already knew.

Bill looked from Lydia to Ethan to Zoe before clapping. "A brand new Blackwell in the family! Congratulations." He beamed.

Laura and Shena got up to hug Zoe. Excited chatter buzzed around the table.

"One more thing," Ethan added. He got down on one knee next to Zoe and said, "Hopefully that will be two new Blackwells in the family." He picked up the box that the rattle was in and pulled out the most beautiful, radiant diamond ring Zoe had ever laid eyes on.

Her eyes watered. One hand flew to her mouth. "Ethan." Her voice was a tearful whisper.

"Zoe Baldwin. Please say that you'll be my wife."

"Oh, my goodness, Ethan. Yes. Yes. I will be your wife!" She wrapped her arms around Ethan and then kissed him all over his face.

They were in a room full of family members, but at that moment, the only two people in the world were Zoe and the man she was about to spend the rest of her life with.

* * * * *

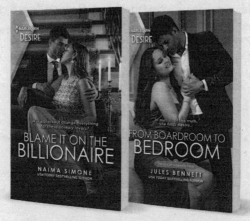

#2785 BACK IN THE TEXAN'S BED

Texas Cattleman's Club: Heir Apparent • by Naima Simone
When Charlotte Jarrett returns to Royal, Texas, with a child, no one's more surprised than her ex-lover, oil heir Ross Edmond. Determined to claim his son, he entices her to move in with him. But can rekindled passion withstand the obstacles tearing them apart?

#2786 THE HEIR

Dynasties: Mesa Falls • by Joanne Rock
To learn the truth about the orphaned boy she's raising, Nicole Cruz takes a job at Mesa Falls Ranch. Co-owner Desmond Pierce has his own suspicions and vows to provide for them. But he didn't expect the complication of a red-hot attraction to Nicole...

#2787 SCANDALIZING THE CEO

Clashing Birthrights • by Yvonne Lindsay
Falsely accused of embezzlement, executive assistant Tami Wilson is forced into spying on her boss, CEO Keaton Richmond, to prove her innocence. But it isn't long until their professional relationship turns very personal. What happens when Keaton learns the truth...?

#2788 ONE NIGHT WITH CINDERELLA

by Niobia Bryant
Shy housekeeper Monica Darby has always had feelings for handsome chef and heir to his family's fortune Gabe Cress. But one unexpected night of passion and a surprise inheritance change everything. With meddling families and painful pasts, will they find their happily-ever-after?

#2789 SEDUCING HIS SECRET WIFE

Redhawk Reunion • by Robin Covington
A steamy tryst leads to a quickie Vegas wedding for notorious CEO playboy Justin Ling and his best friend's sister, Sarina Redhawk. Then, to please investors and their disapproving families, they continue a fake relationship. Are their feelings becoming all too real?

#2790 TWICE THE TEMPTATION

Red Dirt Royalty • by Silver James
After a hurricane traps storm chaser Brittany Owens with tempting Cooper Tate, tension transforms into passion. But Cooper turns out to be her new boss! As their paths keep crossing, can she keep her promise to remain professional, especially when she learns she's pregnant—with twins?

"Hopefully everyone will get home safe," she said.

Gabe took in her high cheekbones, the soft roundness of her jaw
and the tilt of her chin. The scent of something subtle but sweet
surrounded her. He forced his eyes away from her and cleared his
throat. "Hopefully," he agreed as he poured a small amount of
champagne into his flute.

"I'll leave you to celebrate," Monica said.

With a polite nod, Gabe took a sip of his drink and set the bottle
at his feet, trying to ignore the reasons why he was so aware of her.
Her scent. Her beauty. Even the gentle night winds shifting her
hair back from her face. Distance was best. Over the past week he
had fought to do just that to help his sudden awareness of her ebb.
Ever since the veil to their desire had been removed, it had been
hard to ignore.

She turned to leave, but moments later a yelp escaped her as
her feet got twisted in the long length of her robe and sent her body
careening toward him as she tripped.

Reacting swiftly, he reached to wrap his arm around her waist
and brace her body up against his to prevent her fall. He let the hand
holding his flute drop to his side. Their faces were just precious

inches apart. When her eyes dropped to his mouth, he released a small gasp. His eyes scanned her face before locking with hers.

He knew just fractions of a second had passed, but right then, with her in his arms and their eyes locked, it felt like an eternity. He wondered what it felt like for her. Was her heart pounding? Her pulse sprinting? Was she aroused? Did she feel that pull of desire?

He did.

With a tiny lick of her lips that was nearly his undoing, Monica raised her chin and kissed him. It was soft and sweet. And an invitation.

"Monica?" he asked, heady with desire, but his voice deep and soft as he sought clarity.

"Kiss me," she whispered against his lips, hunger in her voice.

"Shit," Gabe swore before he gave in to the temptation of her and dipped his head to press his mouth down upon hers.

And it was just a second more before her lips and her body softened against him as she opened her mouth and welcomed him with a heated gasp that seemed to echo around them. The first touch of his tongue to hers sent a jolt through his body, and he clutched her closer to him as her hands snaked up his arms and then his shoulders before clutching the lapels of his tux in her fists. He assumed she was holding on while giving in to a passion that was irresistible.

Monica was lost in it all. Blissfully.

The taste and feel of his mouth were everything she ever imagined.

Ever dreamed of.

Ever longed for.

Don't miss what happens next in
One Night with Cinderella
by nationally bestselling author Niobia Bryant!

Available February 2021 wherever
Harlequin Desire books and ebooks are sold.

Harlequin.com

HDEXP0121